Val J.

My Home
Street Home

My Home
Street Home

A Novel

Val Stevens

iUniverse, Inc.
New York Lincoln Shanghai

My Home Street Home

iUniverse books may be ordered through booksellers or by contacting:

iUniverse
2021 Pine Lake Road, Suite 100
Lincoln, NE 68512
www.iuniverse.com
1-800-Authors (1-800-288-4677)

Because of the dynamic nature of the Internet, any Web addresses or links contained in this book may have changed since publication and may no longer be valid.

This is a work of fiction. All of the characters, names, incidents, organizations, and dialogue in this novel are either the products of the author's imagination or are used fictitiously.

ISBN: 978-0-595-47473-8 (pbk)
ISBN: 978-0-595-71111-6 (cloth)
ISBN: 978-0-595-91745-7 (ebk)

Printed in the United States of America

This story is dedicated to "Honey," who regrettably didn't come back to Edmonton's downtown in the summer of 2007, and the "City Hall Lady," both people of the streets who provided my inspiration.

Many thanks for support and assistance to Lorraine Wadel; Margot Crane; Shannon Crane; Wendy Campbell; my husband, Andy Maguire; and others who encouraged me to "get that story out there."

Cover photography: Michael James, www.michaeljames.ca

One

It's quite chilly this morning. I can smell winter in the air.

Eddie always teased me about my thing with smells. "What do you mean, it smells blue? Blue doesn't smell."

Of course it does. Blue smells like starched cotton, with a slight hint of pepper. And winter smells like baking soda, very dry and subtle but distinct.

It's always cooler here in the ravine, so I pack up for the day, thinking it will be warmer at street level. Mill Creek cuts a deep slash through this part of the city, a remnant of the last retreating ice age. Its network of parks department trails is popular with runners and bikers, but few of those trails dip down to the actual creek bed. The times I've stood on rocks in the middle of the creek and watched the water tumble past, I've imagined there must be remnants of that old glacier hiding out to this day.

Other than the trails and a few picnic sites, the ravine is pretty much isolated wilderness in the middle of a large city. When you stand on Mill Creek Bridge, the valley floor is hundreds of feet below you, and our campsites impossible to see.

I'm still okay in this so far mild fall weather, what with my blankets and being off the ground, but when it gets colder, I'll have to rethink my situation.

It's just Mr. Taylor and me left now. Betty is in jail or rehab, we're not sure where. She went on a serious drunk a few weeks ago, did a lot of damage at a martini bar. She assaulted a couple of young women with a broken glass and left in hand cuffs, according to what we heard.

The parks ranger people came down a few days ago and packed up and pulled down her camp site. I wish I'd known they were coming. I wanted to go ask if I could have her tent, but Mr. Taylor said it was better that we didn't attract attention to ourselves.

Luke's gone to Vancouver. The young actor he met during the Fringe Festival turned out to be as serious about Luke as he is about theatre. When the curtain fell on his last act, he came down to the ravine with two bus tickets to the west coast and helped Luke pack his few possessions. I'm happy for Luke that he found someone special. He always seemed so alone, even when he was with all of us.

Hannah, who always seemed put on to me, admitted her parents had been begging her to come home for a long time now. So much for the story about tough love and being driven to the streets. She left two days ago. I think for Hannah this summer was all about making a statement. Earning some cachet in whatever social circles she runs in: driven out by her parents, forced to live on the streets, then back home on her own terms with highly repentant mom and dad.

Mr. Taylor has plans, too. He's eligible for his senior's pension in September and thinks he will find a boarding house for the winter. He says the winters are getting too hard on his old bones, although, overall, he prefers life outside "the system," as he calls it.

I'm the only one without plans.

I'm thinking about my day as I pack. I'm sure I've worn out my welcome on the east stretch of Whyte Avenue. I've been to the same restaurant two days in a row now; neither day have they had any work. Normally, the staff happily let me break down boxes, haul out garbage, other jobs they don't want to do. There's no money in it, though; just a coffee and yesterday's pastry or a sandwich. But they seem to be tiring of my presence, so I'll move on west today.

School is back in, so I could go over to the high school. That's Betty's brain child. She's quite resourceful, like knowing many high school kids throw their mom-made lunches in the garbage before going into school and instead eat in the school cafeteria. At Scona High last week, I rescued three lunches almost before they settled in the can. The ham sandwiches stayed fresh in my cooler for a couple days. I still have an apple I'll eat next time I find a salt package. Eddie thought it was weird to put salt on my apples. I told him it draws out the flavour, like it does with tomatoes.

Eddie and I loved eating ripe beefeaters off the vine with the sunshine still on them. We'd pass the salt shaker back and forth, tomato juice running up to our elbows and dripping on the patio table. Those were such good times, the years with Eddie. How did everything go so wrong in the end? How will I ever stop missing him?

Ready now, I step over my "fence." The trip wires were Hannah's idea. We circled a generous area around our private spaces with ankle high rope; that way, anyone coming close in the dark would run into them, making ample noise as they stumbled or fell, and we'd have fair warning of intruders. No one had ever breached my space, but Hannah caught two people this summer, a couple of kids sneaking around past their curfew. Both had fallen quite heavily and left, muttering and moaning, with no need to shoo them off.

Part way up the path, I peek through the bushes to see if Mr. Taylor has left yet. No, looks like he's still asleep. Then I notice his camp is disturbed: books and other things are flung around the little clearing. Things look wrong.

I move closer. Things are terribly wrong.

Mr. Taylor is lying in a heap, not moving, even when I call his name. I bend over him and see that his face is covered in dried blood, his eyes wide open. There's a bloody rock a few feet away. His luggage cart is flung against a tree, broken. And I know Mr. Taylor is dead.

I start to shake in terror, backing slowly toward the cover of the bushes, checking to see if anyone is still around.

No, whoever did this is long gone.

His fanny pack is missing. The only things in it were grad pictures of his children and a faded, tissue-thin newspaper clipping from his 25th wedding anniversary. He never kept his money with him, and I realize now I don't know where he hid it. Whoever killed him netted a few pieces of paper worth nothing to anyone but Mr. Taylor.

I pick up one of his precious books, flung in the dirt, stomped on, kicked around. My stomach empties, but the gagging continues until I'm dizzy and barely able to walk. And I decide to get out of here now. The ravine is no longer a safe place; I need to get away.

The climb up the steep path from the ravine tires me. Rush hour is just beginning as I cross Mill Creek Bridge and hit the avenue. I'm still shaking and my mind is jumping from thought to thought: if only Mr. Taylor didn't read by flashlight after dark, acting like a beacon in the darkness, would he still be alive? Should I go to the police, or would that only draw attention to me, open up a bunch of questions I couldn't or wouldn't want to answer?

Where would I go tonight, not feeling safe in the valley anymore? Why didn't Eddie take care of things like he said he was going to? Why did this have to happen to me?

I plunk down on a bus bench and let my tears flow. I sob for Mr. Taylor, for Eddie, for myself. Life just seems damn unfair sometimes.

TWO

Like anyone, I had had great dreams of a successful career, a great lifestyle, heaps of money. But I went to work right after high school, helping my mom put my brothers through university. I always thought, when they graduated, I'd move to a city, maybe Regina or even Toronto, take night courses and get better and better jobs as time went on.

Then Mom got sick. Cancer. I felt it was her right to stay in her home for as long as she wanted. She had raised three children on her own and we never missed out on much, but it took a lot of hard work and sacrifice on her part. Both my brothers had lives in other cities so that left me to move in and take care of her.

When she died, after an ordeal of pain and depression that threatened to suck the life out of me as well, I was content just to drift for a while. There wasn't a great variety of job opportunities in my small town, but I found steady work. The job at the hardware turned into the job at the insurance company that turned into the one at the law office. I hadn't met anyone I wanted a second date with, never mind spend my life with. Mind you, the playing field wasn't very big and most people in town were either married or gone to a city by that age.

I kept busy with a few friends, writing poetry and trying to get published, surrounded by books and notepads. I just slipped into an easy routine and it felt comfortable. I was surprised when I turned 40; where had all the time gone? But I could imagine a similarly quiet retirement, living on a small pension, content with a couple of cats and a long reading list.

Then I met Eddie and my life turned around completely. We were passionate about trying new things, being open to change. But nothing could have prepared me for the change that happened one afternoon a few months ago.

I don't know where I'd be now if it weren't for Mr. Taylor. He quite literally saved my life.

Mr. Taylor found me at the beginning of the summer, after a night when I'd tried sleeping in an apartment parkade and was kicked out by a security guard. I finally found refuge on the back porch of a hair salon; I put my purse down for a pillow and tried to scrunch as much of me as possible into my jacket. Red streaks were just showing in the morning sky when a soft whisper woke me. "Hello there. What's a fine lady like you doing sleeping in the garden?" I woke to see the face of an older man peering at me through the slats of the porch railing.

Surprise and the gentleness of his tone undid me: I burst out crying. Without a second thought, I poured out to this total stranger the whole sordid tale of how I came to be sleeping on this porch.

The man listened patiently, clucking with sympathy here, gasping in surprise there. When I finished, he shook his head for a long time, pulling thoughtfully on his beard.

"What a ghastly experience. How could anyone treat a fellow human in such an abominable manner? It's a scandal, just a complete shame."

He patted my hand. "First things first. I do think you could use a coffee. I'll walk up the street and get some, then we can figure out what you need to do." I stared at his outstretched palm for a moment, then dug in my purse for some money.

He walked off, wheeling a loaded luggage cart behind him, and was back in moments with two steaming coffees. Nothing ever smelled so good to me before.

"Now, let us think this through. You say you can't go home, but what about friends? Is there someone who can put you up for a few days until you get things straightened out?"

I didn't have to think about it. "No, there's no one." At one time, I would have simply gone straight to Anna's house, or one of the other lunch ladies. But I'm pretty sure none of them would show me any sympathy after what happened. Besides, I'd be too ashamed to beg help from them.

"Then, my dear, I'm afraid you will be joining a distinct segment of our society that lives an alternative lifestyle. The first thing is to get you outfitted."

"Outfitted? What do you mean?"

"Well, that suit isn't practical if you're going to live outside. You need warmer clothes and some blankets and necessities."

"What do you mean, live outside? I can't be a … a … a street person. A homeless person!"

"Well, my dear, you've only just told me you have no home to go to. It is unfortunate as can be and completely out of your control, but I'm afraid for the time being you are indeed a homeless person."

I guess, whenever I thought of homeless people, I always thought of drunks, druggies, people who were too lazy to work. Stereotypical perceptions. People who had done something or lacked something or, whatever, to deserve the life they led. I was starting to see things in a whole new light. One minute, I was smug and complacent about my good fortune in life, looking at people without homes with a certain benevolent distaste, the next minute, the unthinkable: I'm one of them.

I started to sob again, but the man cut me off short.

"Now crying won't help you," he said. "But I can. I've been doing this lifestyle for a long time, so I can help you get set up nicely and you can stay with us in the ravine."

"Us? Who's us?"

"Just a few folks like you and me who look out for each other. We have a nice place over by Mill Creek culvert, and nobody bothers us. The park rangers know we're there, but they look the other way as long as there's no trouble. We have an empty space right now because Terry picked a fight with a police officer last week. He won't be back any time soon. That boy never could hold his temper, and the officer was just talking to him, asking a few questions."

"Look, mister …"

"Mr. Robert Taylor. No relation to the movie star."

"Right. Mr. Taylor. Thanks and all, but I'm not living near some culvert. I applied for a bunch of jobs up Whyte yesterday and I'm going back to see about them today. Right now, as a matter of fact."

"That is excellent, my dear. Why don't I just tag along with you? I'm headed that way myself. Best time to find bottles is early in the day. If I locate an ample supply, I can return the favour of a coffee later on."

He talked as we walked.

"Unpleasant as it may be, you just have to face facts, dear woman. You are here through no fault of your own, but it doesn't change the fact of your situation. At least you don't have to blame yourself for this trouble."

"What do you mean?" I asked.

"I'm here through my own stupidity. I have no one to blame but myself. You at least can carry yourself with pride, instead of feeling like an old drunk who threw it all away."

"An old drunk?" I replied. "You seem like a perfectly respectable, well-educated gentleman."

"That may appear true, which is why my downfall is so much more a disgrace than that of someone who perhaps came from a bad background and never had a real chance in life. Because, once, I had it all."

He looked off to the side as he spoke, and I knew what he was telling me shamed him. He spoke of a kind and caring wife who immigrated to Canada with him from Britain for the chance of a better career. Of two sons, a daughter. A respectable job teaching high school literature and a respectable home in a respectable neighbourhood.

"But I liked my alcohol. I pretended to myself the drinking was harmless; my colleagues drank, but unlike me, they knew when to stop. Mornings were becoming tough to face. My wife tried to talk to me, begged me to get help, but I was looking at the world through the bottom of a glass.

"The school board finally got tired of my hangovers and public drunkenness, and 'retired' me on a small pension. Even then, the drinking didn't stop. I drank until I lost my house. I drank until I lost my wife, until my children wouldn't see me anymore.

"I was completely 'blotto' the night I staggered in front of a bus. I was unconscious in the hospital for 48 hours. When I woke up, the driver of said bus was sitting beside my bed, weeping with joy. She was a pretty little thing, and one of the city's best drivers, but running me down had broken her spirit. She could never drive bus again, she said.

"Nothing I said made a difference; she was leaving the job and going back home to her little farming hometown, to Calmar or somewhere.

"That's when I realized how many lives I'd ruined, besides my own. I cried through the next four days until they released me.

"I had nowhere to go. No relatives, no friends who would talk to me, nobody but my own foolish company. I was down to my last eight dollars. My landlord had evicted me from the rooming house the afternoon I was hit by the bus.

"I departed the hospital with a mission: the nearest liquor store for a bottle of wine. I just walked down Whyte taking tugs off the bottle, waiting for oblivion to set in. After about six blocks, I realized I hated the taste of the alcohol and threw it away. And I just walked and walked and walked while I acknowledged I had hit rock bottom, lost everything."

Not quite everything, Mr. Taylor. You had something left—your dignity, your soul, your life—but last night someone took even that from you.

Three

A few passers-by stare curiously as I sit and cry. Time to move on before someone gets too curious or, worse, calls for help.

One of Mr. Taylor's tips for street life: Always walk with purpose, as though you have a clear destination you are looking forward to. Difficult as that is today, I stand tall and walk off with determination.

The street I turn down is quiet. Best to stay away from the main avenue until rush hour quiets down. Especially until I can get these tears under control. There's a bench over by the fire hall; I'll sit there until I can pull myself together.

Mr. Taylor and I made slow progress that morning we first met. As we walked down Whyte Avenue to the places where I'd left job applications, Mr. Taylor stopped at every garbage can to search for bottles and cans. Once he even ran across the avenue, dodging cars, because he saw a box of beer bottles by the curb. He came back triumphant. "Only two broken! That's a fine start to the day."

He stashed them in an upscale shopping bag attached to his luggage cart.

By then, we'd reached the trendy part of Whyte Avenue. The next eight blocks or so are called Old Strathcona and are a local favourite: the historic buildings are protected by civic bylaws and contain a funky array of book stores, clothing shops, coffee places, unique gift stores and hemp outfitters. And of course the bars, many featuring live music.

We stopped at the first store where I'd answered the "help wanted" poster. A different woman was there today and I asked her about the job. It was filled yesterday, she said. Nice young girl, just moved to town, eager to get to work.

The next job was filled too, and the next.

At the fourth place, the manager looked me over with hands on her hips, taking in my expensive suit. "Look honey, no offence, but this bar can get pretty rough. I don't think this is your kind of crowd. Maybe try a nice dress shop or a book store."

I made it out without crying, but barely. Mr. Taylor was waiting patiently for me, an eager look on his face.

"No." That was all I said.

There was one last application to check. I spoke to the girl at the front counter and she picked up the phone. "Someone here about the job." A few minutes later, a young man in stylish black with a shaved head and multiple earrings approached me.

"Um, look ma'am." I wanted to scream at him: don't call me ma'am like I'm some old person. I wasn't even 50 yet.

"Look around this place. What do you see? All those computer monitors? This is an Internet café, and one of the jobs is to keep those computers running. I really don't think you're what we're looking for; we want somebody younger and computer savvy." He began to walk away.

"Wait! I can learn. I ran computers at the feed store, keeping tabs on inventory," I pled.

"No, sorry, you just won't do."

Mr. Taylor knew the answer from the look on my face. He took my arm and led me to the lights at the corner.

"Now don't be too disappointed. You can try again tomorrow. Meanwhile, let's get you accessorized. We have a ways to go. Do you have bus fare?" I nodded, and paid both his and my fare when we boarded. He took two transfers and set off for the back of the bus headed to Bonnie Doon Mall.

Our first stop was the mall's dollar superstore.

"Speak to me loudly about bungee cords, pretend you can't find them. And open your purse." I did what he said, and gasped in horror when he dropped a flashlight into my purse. Next were a package of batteries, a four-pack of disposable lighters and a travel mug. My purse was getting full, and I hissed at him to stop.

"This is stealing. I can't steal. Stop putting things in."

"You just keep talking about bungee cords." He popped in a length of thick plastic rope next.

Then a cheap fork, spoon and knife, two plastic plates, some tin pie plates and a box of baggies. He motioned me to zip the purse closed.

"Here they are, dear. You walked past the cords three times. Can't see the forest for the trees." He handed me the cords—six for a dollar—and told me to go pay for them.

The clerk took my dollar and six cents, asking if I'd found everything I needed. I was in such a state of shock, I could only nod.

Mr. Taylor followed me out, rolling his cart behind him and humming some show tune. I couldn't believe I'd let him put those things in my purse. I'd never stolen a thing in my life. I imagined the contraband glowing like neon inside my purse, telling everyone I was a thief. I didn't know yet how much of a thief I was going to be before the afternoon was over.

Our next stop was the Safeway at the end of the mall. A store clerk was rolling a huge line of shopping buggies toward the store, with four or five folding carts on top. When the clerk turned to round up a few more buggies, Mr. Taylor grabbed one of the folding carts off the top and told me to run behind the store with it. I shook my head violently, but he pushed me into a run. And I ran.

In a few minutes, he came whistling around the corner, and took my arm to walk me to the avenue.

"Ideally, one would want a luggage rack like my own, but they are not as easy to come by. The shopping cart will have to do. And much better than one of those big grocery buggies; they simply scream 'homeless person,' don't you think?

"Onward, my dear, to the thrift shop, to select an appropriate wardrobe and your boudoir linens." He was acting such a rascal, I burst out laughing. My situation was certainly no joke, but with Mr. Taylor I was almost enjoying myself. Besides, this is only temporary, I thought. When I get back on my feet again, things will be different.

Up and down the aisles of the thrift shop we went while Mr. Taylor urged me to choose from assorted blankets and towels, plus some small travel bags to hold my worldly goods. I found a queen size fleecy bed cover in golds and black with a growling lion's head on it. "Just the thing to protect you during the night," he insisted. I protested at the price, but he just helped me refold it, and placed it in the shopping buggy.

Next was the clothing aisle where I chose a few outfits: a warm sweater, a quilted vest and three pairs of casual pants. The buggy was almost full when he handed me a plastic rain poncho.

"Here, pay for this item, and I'll meet you behind the store." I had no idea what he was up to but I gave the cashier four dollars for the rain gear and walked out.

I didn't see Mr. Taylor at first, then his head popped around the corner of the thrift shop. I followed him to the back where a door was propped open and thousands of cigarette butts littered the pavement. And where the shopping buggy was sitting, full of the things he'd help me select.

"Those store clerks shouldn't smoke so much. They will make themselves ill," he told me. "Now grab everything you can hold, I'll get the rest, and go over behind that hedge there." I did as he told me.

He joined me in a moment and instructed me in the fine art of rolling, folding, packing and strapping stolen goods to the cart. He tore off every price tag, and left them in a small heap under the hedge. I pointed out to him we had roughly one hundred dollars worth of liberated articles.

"And have you not yourself sent unwanted items to this, that or other charities? Consider it pay back, then, and let us move along."

Our next stop was the back of a donair shop where the chief cook and bottle washer would, Mr. Taylor said, sell us a bag of day-old hoagie buns for a quarter. The cook would tell the owner that he'd thrown the buns out. The quarter went in the cook's pocket, the buns to a good home, and nobody got hurt.

"Where are we going next?"

"For a stroll down the lane, dear. Just a nice stroll down the lane."

The stroll down the residential lane netted us a two-litre milk jug, put out for recycling, which we washed and filled at a tap behind a garage, and a child's plastic pail, just right for washing one's dainties, he said. The thought of Mr. Taylor washing dainties cracked me up. I laughed so hard, I had to sit down or pee.

"Um, Mr. Taylor, where do we, um, like, 'go'?" I asked.

"Soon, my dear. We just need to get into the ravine first." And he veered off behind the brick youth shelter and followed a path that led down into a valley.

I followed him down a paved walking trail, through rough paths in dense bush, past a municipal outdoor pool—"Cheapest shower and laundry in town, and for the price of admission, you can use the barbeque grills should you encounter a steak at some time"—and onward and under the bridge. We stopped by a thick grove of shrubbery and he indicated the way to the "facilities."

The facilities turned out to be the bush of my choice.

As we carried on, the lack of sleep last night was getting to me. I was so tired I kept stumbling, but he assured me we were almost there.

And then we were. "There" was a small clearing with a rickety picnic table and a stove of sorts atop a metal pole. The patchy grass looked newly raked, and a small pile of sticks and paper was carefully stacked beside the fire. A smudge fire was burning to ward off mosquitoes. Now I appreciated Mr. Taylor's liberation of several bottles of DEET at the discount store.

But that was it. It didn't look like home to me.

"But where do you stay," I asked in a whining tone. "You don't just sleep out here in the open, do you?"

"Ah, be patient. One must observe social amenities before demanding a bed for the night." He walked over to a partly hidden path and called out. "Betty, are you home? I have someone for you to meet." A voice answered and we started toward it.

Four

A siren starts up and the fire rescue truck roars out of the garage, turning toward Mill Creek Bridge. Has someone found Mr. Taylor? I could tell them there's no need to rush.

The tears start up again, thinking about Mr. Taylor, missing the companionship of the ravine community. How I miss that, though at the time I thought I'd sunk as low as a person can go.

I liked Betty the minute I saw her. She was exotic, a gypsy type, with a soft, sweet face and compassionate blue eyes. She moved with such elegance that no one would presume to call her fat. She wore a lavish collection of layers, a brilliantly patterned pashmina over a tiered skirt, an embroidered vest and multi-layered tops in peacock colours, teal, jade and emerald. A large lapis lazuli pendant swung as she moved. She took my hands between her own gentle ones and welcomed me warmly to the camp.

Behind Betty was a small tent, the overhang edged with long fringes in colours as vibrant as her clothes. The tent sat up on pallets, which I later learned were the god-send of homeless camps. A piece of indoor-outdoor carpet lay in front of the tent door. Bright shawls and cushions adorned a bamboo papasan chair with a matching footstool. Something savoury bubbled on a small hibachi and marigolds and daisies tumbled out of two clay pots. I found myself thinking, "Nice set-up," before I realized this was about a person who lived in a tent in a ravine.

I would later spend hours with Betty, talking, sharing memories, despairing of the cruelty some people displayed—like Eddie's kids. I could hardly believe it later when Mr. Taylor told me she was a drunk, a mean, vicious drunk who could tear people apart and later forget the horrid things she'd said. I saw it only once, but it scared me so badly I left the camp for three days, waiting for her to get sober.

Mr. Taylor briefly explained my situation before asking Betty if I could stay with them for a while.

"It's just for a while," I insisted. "I'll get a job and save up for a damage deposit, and get my life together again."

I saw the look that flashed between Betty and Mr. Taylor. They knew what I didn't then—working while you're homeless is a huge challenge, and with most of the jobs I'd be able to get, it would take months to save enough money.

Betty agreed I could stay, and, later, so did Luke Higley. Luke claimed to be the great-great grandson of Brewster Higley, the man who wrote Home, Home on the Range. Luke had his own version of the song:
"Home, home on the range,
Where the bums and the derelicts play.
Where never is heard an encouraging word
And the sky rains on beggars all day."
He was funny and smart, and I liked him right away. It was almost as if I knew him from somewhere. We got along fine.

Hannah, the last member of the camp, was another story. It was mutual dislike at first glance. She was a Goth caricature, right out of central casting. She resented the attention Mr. Taylor paid to me and stomped around the clearing in her beat-up Dr. Martens, muttering under her breath. Just looking at her made my stomach roll. She had small safety pins fastened along the edge of one earlobe and the other lobe was stretched wide, with no flesh in the centre, by a thing like a grommet. I've never been able to stomach facial piercings, and these were worse than most.

Hannah was the only one of us with a job; she worked as a shampoo girl at an alternative salon four days a week. The pay wasn't enough for an apartment, and she spent much of it on supplies to keep her hair in rigid, punk spikes. Truthfully, I couldn't stand to be near her. Of course, she sensed that right off and went out of her way to get in my face. When she was around, I spent a lot of time in my "loft." But she reluctantly agreed I could stay, as long as I didn't "go around acting like some big shot."

We shared the clearing, but everyone had a private spot in the surrounding greenery. Mine was called the loft because Terry, the one who had fought the policeman and was in jail, fastened together a platform of pallets and suspended the construction from the limbs of a huge tree. It was only two feet off the ground, but that distance kept the damp and chill away. The walls and roof were branches of smaller trees, lashed together painstakingly to form a living barrier. Terry left behind a small supply of painters' drop sheets to throw over the roof if it rained.

About a week after I met Mr. Taylor and the rest, I took a bus trip back to the house where I'd lived with Eddie. I could see the For Sale sign as soon as I turned onto our street, but was shocked when I got closer to see a Sold sticker already.

I walked past the house until I got to the alley, then doubled back to the rear. About eight huge garbage bags were stacked by the back gate, and I could see my tatami mats sticking out of a garbage can. As I pulled them out to rescue them, a car came toward me. I held my breath until it passed; it was a neighbour from the far end of the block. I doubt he recognized me.

I wanted to see what was in the bags; in my mind, I visualized Eddie's daughters pitching everything I owned into the garbage. The first held books and some older towels. They probably kept the new ones.

The second was a hodgepodge: CDs, a few smaller prints, some kitchen items. I rescued my shampoo and body wash and tucked them in one of my duffle bags.

As I began to open the third, I heard the gate open next door. Mrs. Diotka, probably. I quickly hid between the garage and the fence; I didn't want a scene with her. She dumped something in a metal can and returned to her house.

Returning to the third bag, I discovered a few items of my clothing. These I bundled away too.

The fourth bag made me cry. Right at the top were a few rolls of undeveloped film, pulled out of the canister and exposed. Deliberately ruined. These were probably our vacation shots from Hawaii. How heartless; I was stunned at such deliberate disregard for others' feelings.

I picked a few other usable items but soon had all I could carry. At least they could have sent the stuff to the Sally Ann. But apparently it was all trash to them, dispensable, like me.

Always a renovator, the next day I thumb tacked two of the tatami mats to the suspended platform and another to the pallet that served as a "doormat." I rigged a rope and green garbage bag over a limb, like a pulley with a knot at the end, to store things I didn't want to carry with me on the street each day. I lashed a small battery LED light to one of the tree branches; it cast a soft glow that didn't penetrate beyond my small space. It seemed more like my place then. On warm evenings, the smell rising from the grass mats lulled me to sleep.

Funny. Eddie and I used to visit back and forth with a few couples, and we always came home laughing about their need to fill
every square inch of their homes with furniture, overdone art work
and tsotchkes. We liked our spare, minimalist home with the bare
hardwood and grass mats, the simply framed art and low slung
leather sofas. I wondered what he'd think of this spare and minimal
living space.

Eddie and I and another couple went camping one weekend. I
hated it: the dirt, the inconvenience, the bending and crouching to
find supplies or get in and out of the tent. And especially the outdoor
bathrooms. I swore I would never camp again. Now look at me: a
small nook in a ravine, everything I own strapped to a cart and I'm
delighted over some cheap tatami mats. Who'd-a guessed?

Five

I think I have the crying under control now. Stop thinking about Mr. Taylor, I warn myself, and wipe my eyes on my sleeve.

I cut into the alley behind the first of the restaurants and clubs on Whyte. Everything is quiet; these places don't open until noon. I rest for a bit, leaning on the back wall of an auto body shop. Inside, I can hear the whirl of sanders and clanging machinery, and the vent overhead is pouring out welcome heat. The ground is littered with cigarette butts. If there had been anything about Eddie I would have changed, it would have been his smoking.

Actually, though, it was smoking that brought us together.

I met Eddie Weston when he was in town for a conference. I was bartending that night as a favour to a friend. The conference was shutting down when he came over to ask where he could buy cigarettes at that time of night.

The store I recommended was on my way home, and I needed cream for the morning, so we walked over together.

He had the cigarettes open before we left the store. He offered me one, and though I don't smoke, I took it. We lit up and propped ourselves against the store's bicycle rack and started to talk.

He noticed a bar sign down the street and suggested we head over for last call. For some reason, I felt daring and young and happy, so I agreed.

Turned out, we had time for two drinks. I had his business card by the time the bar closed, and we decided we must have known each other from some time before. We had so much in common, and liked many of the same things. He was impressed that I'd had some poetry published and was looking forward to reading my work.

Eddie walked me to my suite three blocks away and asked for my phone number. He was in town often, he said, and he'd like to see me again. Inside my suite, I swooned against the closed door and slid to the floor.

I was like a giddy young girl in the heat of a crush. I waited for his phone call for a week, two weeks, then decided I'd been a fool and cried myself to sleep for a few nights. I was just getting over my piti-fuls when my phone rang one night. It was Eddie, coming to town tomorrow and offering a steak dinner with dancing at the legion after. The giddy young girl took over and made me say yes.

Thus began a year that followed a set pattern. We went out every time Eddie came to town, which was about every three weeks. Usu-ally, we had dinner, sampling the town's somewhat limited culinary offerings. Eddie would tell me about new restaurants in Edmonton, where he lived, and how I had to come to visit and we'd go to a great Japanese-fusion place he knew of, or try the new steakhouse that his friends swore was "the best." Our dinners invariably lasted until the staff was ready to go home; we just had so much to talk about. He was genuinely sad when I told him about my mother, and I sympa-thized with him over the loss of his wife a few years earlier. He always spoke of his children, now grown and living on their own, with such pride, saying they'd love me, he couldn't wait for us to meet.

We grew fonder of each other with every date, but every evening ended in, "See you in a few weeks."

Then Eddie called one night from Regina; he would be in town the next day and could we order in at my place instead of going out? He said we needed to talk. I was nervous right off. Eddie had never been to my suite; we always went out. And the "We need to talk" sounded way too serious.

The next evening, I dusted the coffee table and TV stand three times, changed twice, inspected the bathroom for stray pubes or other signs of neglect and worried myself sick. "We need to talk." I was preparing myself for the worst when there was a knock on the door.

I was nearly bowled over by a huge bouquet of flowers and a bag of wine. Eddie let everything slip to the floor and went on like a crazy man: he admitted he hadn't had any business in town for the past four months, he just came to see me whenever he could find some spare time, which wasn't often enough to please him. He missed me so much in between visits and this wasn't working and why didn't I just leave everything and come to Edmonton to live with him?

He was talking so fast I didn't realize he was getting me half naked in the doorway, in full view of anyone passing by. He finally pulled me into the bedroom and, well, my oh my.

Later—yeah, like in one of those romance novels that skip the details but leave you knowing it was hot and heavy—Eddie went on with his speech.

"I can't think of anything but you, and the next time I can make it down here. I want you to come with me, live with me. Please say yes. I won't go until you do."

I tried to put up a lot of protest, but he had me from "Please say yes." My mental bags were packed. I was going to Edmonton with Eddie and that was that.

My one condition was that I'd leave most of my stuff in storage in case it didn't work out.

It worked out.

Mostly.

A crash and bang up the alley grabs my attention.

Four doors up, a skinny young man is pushing a box of empty liquor bottles out the door with his foot. On one shoulder is a box crammed with kitchen debris. He's obviously going to throw it in the dumpster. No. What can I do to stop him? Dumpster dipping is not my favourite activity.

"Eeeee! Ooooooh. Help. Help me."

The young man drops the box and runs over to me. "Are you okay, lady? Should I call someone?"

I moan a little more and he drops to a squat beside me. I take a quick peek through my screwed up eyes. He looks like a nice, concerned young person.

"I'm … fine. Or I will be in a minute," panting a little to add drama to the situation. When I see him looking around for help, I reach for his hand.

"There were two men chasing me. I ran back here as fast as I could and I fell on my knee. I think it's bleeding." How easily the lies come to me now.

He looks relieved that I'm not having an attack or something and tells me to hold on; he'll go find a first aid kit. There's one somewhere in the nightclub, but it might take a few minutes.

The second the door closes behind him; I go into action. First I drag the box of kitchen waste and hide it behind the concrete block fence across the alley. Then I rummage in my bag until I find an empty bottle with a lid. Squatting, I pour the remaining dribs from the liquor bottles into it, careful not to miss a drop. When I hear footsteps rushing back to the door, I stow my bottle and stand to greet the young man holding a handful of dusty band-aids in his hand.

"Thanks dear, but it's not bleeding after all. I think I'm fine and thank you for your kindness." I leave him looking after me as I retrieve my cart. As soon as I hear the door close, I rush behind the fence to the box.

Well, it's my lucky day. Two generous heels of bread, one French and a rye. A stub of corned beef that a sniff tells me is still quite fresh. The rest is vegetable scraps that might make a kind of soup: chunks of carrot and potatoes, the ends of a celery bunch and one whole perfect onion. The things some people throw out!

Quickly I hide everything in my cooler bag and bungee cord all my parcels to the cart. Another of Mr. Taylor's tips for street life: don't flash your riches around. The person watching may be more desperate than you. I can feel tears starting again; time to get moving.

I plan to go down into the river valley to Queen Elizabeth Park. The park has picnic sites with outdoor grills I can use to cook my meal, plus a great view of the North Saskatchewan River. Eddie always said a drink or two and a good meal could salvage even a miserable day, and wasn't this just one of the most miserable days ever. I'm looking forward to cooking a little dinner while I sip my "cocktail du dregs." It can't be any worse than some of the shooters people ordered when I worked at the steakhouse.

Six

I'm thinking back to early summer and day two of job hunting as I walk. I woke early and dressed in my suit without exposing any part of me. So there was some value to Grade 10 gym class after all: being able to remove one outfit and replace it with another without showing a strip of skin. Call me a prude, but I'm not into public nudity. As if there was any public around in the shelter of my ... my what? Hideout? Sanctuary? Home away from home? I could see a whole new vocabulary was required for these living conditions. Thank god it was only for a short time. I'd soon find a job and an apartment and get my life back on track.

Mr. Taylor knew about my plans and we'd agreed to meet at noon in the gazebo park in Old Strathcona. I bought a paper from a news box and was half way into Starbucks for a latte when I remembered I had less than 30 dollars to my name. Maybe the no-name coffee shop down the street better suited my current income bracket.

There were lots of jobs in the classifieds, but I narrowed them down to those close to Whyte Avenue. I didn't want to spend all my wages on bus fare, after all. And I wasn't going to look downtown. Eddie had worked downtown, along with many of his friends, and we spent a lot of time there, at the theatre, the concert hall, the various restaurants and shops. I didn't want to take the chance that I'd run into someone we knew and have to explain what had happened. No, I was better off on the south side where I didn't know many people, where I could blend in and not be noticed.

I circled three or four ads that looked interesting. After a quick clean up in the coffee shop washroom—I realized personal hygiene was going to be an issue—I headed out to apply for the positions.

At the first place, a trendy Italian bistro, the girl at the front desk just told me to leave my resume and they'd get back to me. I was stunned; I'd never had a resume. In my town, where everybody knew most everybody, employers knew your job credentials, what your previous boss thought of you and what they might get away with paying you.

I must have looked stunned because the girl nonchalantly said, "Run out of copies? You can print a few up at the library for cheap." I returned her smile and replied to her.

"How silly of me. Actually, I left my printouts on the kitchen counter. That's why I looked so dozy."

"Sure. Well, bring one back and we'll see."

I left in a hurry. Out on the street, I figured there was nothing to do but head for the library. The brick building was a historical site, but I knew it had up-to-date computers.

Two hours later, I had printed a reasonable enough account of my work experience. I emphasized my stints as a club hostess and bartender; most of the jobs I'd seen in the paper were service industry positions. As I paid the librarian for the copies, she noted I had two overdue books. Another shock went through me. Those books were at Eddie's, or in the trash, if I knew his daughters. Unless I brought them back, I'd lose my library privileges.

Making up a quick story about losing the books on a trip, I asked to pay the replacement cost. Between that and the copies, I walked out with less than $10 to my name. I really needed a job now; my money wasn't going to last long at this rate.

When I returned to the bistro, the girl smiled at me apologetically. "Sorry, the manager just hired someone a few minutes ago."

I'm sure dejection lit me like a neon sign. But she came around the desk and said in a low voice, "My friend works at the steak place around the corner? And they're looking for staff?" I almost hugged her as I rushed out the door.

As I headed down the street, I saw Greenwoods' Book Shoppe across from me. Now there's a store I'd like to work in, I thought. I had been a frequent browser at Greenwoods II downtown, and I had once shared a table with Laurie Greenwood at a fundraising event. There would be too much explaining to do about why I was looking for work and where Eddie was, so I carried on to my destination.

Within half an hour, I was employed. Mack, the lounge manager, hired me on as the lunch bartender, 11 to 3, Tuesday to Saturday, serving the lunch crowd and getting the bar ready for happy hour. Best of all, early staff got to finish the lunch specials before leaving for the day. The pay wasn't that great, but Mack said tips could be good and weren't shared among all staff like in most places.

"It's mostly business people at lunch and they tip better than the kids and students who come for happy hour and the evening."

We agreed I'd start the next day, and I left on two feet of air. I had a job in a great restaurant, and one meal a day was taken care of. Things were looking up.

Seven

A car stops to let me cross the street, its window open and the weather forecast blaring out.

"Get out your toasty pj's; we're dropping to minus 18 by midnight. Tomorrow we'll see snow by suppertime, with high winds and blizzard warnings in effect for the Edmonton area. Hope you've all got your snow tires on, and don't plan on any out-of-town trips. And now the news, brought to you by Edmonton's premiere steak house …" My steak house. Where I'd worked with Mack.

I think about that first job again. I really liked it and Mack seemed pleased with my work. There were a few new cocktails to look up, but thank god I wasn't working the happy hour. Those new shooters the kids loved would have made me crazy: Slippery Nipple, Purple Haze, Blow Job. Most of them sounded obscene; not just the names but the combinations were absurd to a highball mixer and beer puller like me.

My first paycheque was a shock. At what I was making for a week, it would take me months to raise a damage deposit, never mind pay rent on the cheapest suite I could find.

The small paycheque wasn't a problem for long, however. The end came barely four weeks after I started.

I had just served three Martinis and two Caesars at a table of regulars when I noticed a group of men walk in. I almost dropped my tray. It was Dan Portman, Garry Betters and George Wiley, three of Eddie's best friends.

I fled to the small room behind the bar before they could see me, breathless with fear. Mack looked up from his desk in irritation. "What the hell?" He had been in a testy mood for days now; something about the restaurant owner wanting to see higher profit out of the bar. He had gone so far as to suggest substituting cheaper booze and smaller portions, something that drove a professional like Mack nuts. If he wasn't already fit to strangle someone, things would not have turned out like they did.

"Mack, there's some people out there I can't serve. They ... well, I used to know them and, well ... Mack, I just can't go out there."

"What, do you owe them money or something? Come on, get out there and take care of your customers."

"Mack, I can't. I can't face them. You don't understand."

"Well, I think I do understand. You don't want to serve customers, what are you hanging around for?"

"My god, you can't fire me, Mack. I need this job."

"I'm not firing you. I'm saying serve the customers or get out."

It didn't take long to make up my mind. I picked up my purse and left through the service exit. I muttered a curse to Eddie's kids for getting me into this situation.

Eddie and I melded our lifestyles happily. If we weren't entertaining—or being entertained—we would go out for dinner. We tried everything: Thai, Greek, Hungarian, Mexican, Ukrainian, Ethiopian. Most of our favourite spots were downtown, where we'd have dinner before seeing a play or sit with friends after a concert, sharing sinfully rich desserts. My number one treat was the fried breaded cheese at the bistro on Rice Howard. I often met one or another of my new women friends there for lunch.

Other nights we'd watch a rented movie and drink a bottle of wine before going to bed for more of that, "and later, as they lay exhausted …" I teased Eddie that I didn't need to read romance novels, I lived them.

Sounds like perfection, right? There was, though, the typical fly in the ointment. His children.

Eddie's wife had died of cancer. It hadn't been, he said, a particularly close marriage and her death left him without much feeling except for an occasional bout of guilt. She had become pregnant toward the end of high school and they did the right thing: married, had three kids in rapid succession and wound up with nothing to talk about. The kids grew up and moved out and made their own lives. His wife was bored and turned to decorating to occupy her time. The result was a Victorian mini-horror lavished with fussy grapevine wreaths and billowing paisley curtains and bits of lace everywhere and imitation brass ornaments. Eddie said it felt like living in a jewelry box with the lid down.

When she got sick, she didn't linger; from diagnosis to demise was a short six weeks. Eddie said it was merciful, considering how my mother had suffered. For a few weeks after the rather emotionless funeral, the kids hung around, trying to take care of him. They soon caught on that he was strangely relieved rather than bereaved. Their visits tapered off and Eddie carried on with his life.

Eight months later, Eddie and I met.

He told his kids—two daughters and a son—he was seeing someone, but said it barely registered with them. They were that immersed in their own existence and their father lived on the edges of their minds, someone they came to when finances were tight and who got invitations to Thanksgiving and Christmas dinners a day or two before the event, almost as an afterthought.

When I'd been in Edmonton for two months, Eddie thought I should meet his children. We planned a barbeque and the three showed up dutifully and, I thought, curious to see who good old dad had decided to bring into their home. The daughters each brought an elaborate appetizer and the son, a bottle of his homemade wine. All seemed to be going well; they were polite and made easy chitchat and I thought things would be good between us.

I had to slip into the bathroom after dinner. While drying my hands, I heard their voices drift clearly in through the window.

"Can you believe that hair? What, did she scalp Farrah Fawcett to make a wig or something?"

"God, it's her clothes that slay me. Looks like she bought the cast wardrobe from Flashdance. Like, can you even buy leggings any more?"

Give the son credit. He told them to shut up, they were being bitches and I was good company for their dad. And that just set them off again.

"So she moves in here and acts like the slut of the mansion and what? She puts her name on dad's insurance and the house title and—poof—our nice little inheritance is gone?"

"Right, and what did she do with all Mom's pretty things? The house is like Ikea-goes-Asian with all her stupid blinds and grass mats. We better watch out for ourselves; I think she's softened Dad's brain."

I couldn't stand to hear any more. I numbly made it through tea and the carrot cake and said goodbye when they all suddenly had to go—things to do, y'know, catch you later—leaving beer bottles and dishes on the patio and a sinkful of dishes.

After they left, while Eddie was watching the news, I closed myself in the bathroom for a careful look. Maybe the girls were right, I decided; my style could use updating. I looked down at my outfit: an off-the-shoulder tunic and tight Capri pants. Not leggings.

Back home, hockey hair and shags were the norm, but this was the city. Looking like I'm on my way to the Fat Chance Saloon for an evening of line dancing wasn't right here.

I called Anna Franks the next morning. She was delighted to hear my plans, which probably meant a new look was way over due, but she was too polite to say. There was a cancellation at her favourite salon and she booked me for the next day.

There was much oohing and awing over the length of my hair at the salon; three stylists circled me, assessing its weight, discussing bangs, no bangs, blunt cut or layered. Finally, we agreed on a medium bob with "a bit of punk" to it.

The stylist snipped and chopped and razored and cut until there were huge clumps of hair around the chair. He'd taken my glasses when he began to work so I had no idea what he was doing. Then the blow drying and spraying. Finally he handed me my glasses and a mirror.

I was stunned as he twirled the chair to give me a 360 degree look. The cut feathered around my face and chunky layers gave it bounce and a casual feel. I shook my head and it all fell back into place perfectly.

Anna was already waiting for me. The look on her face said it all: now that's an improvement. I felt years younger, and lighter, and more than ready for a shopping trip.

The afternoon was a blur of stores, sales clerks holding up various clothes, fitting rooms and credit card slips. I wound up with several outfits in linen and soft cottons in muted colours I'd never worn before: sage, taupe, ivory, and classic black. I decided to wear one of the new dresses and a pair of strappy high heels to meet Eddie for dinner.

He was already seated when I checked my bags at the front entrance. I walked over and stopped a few feet from his table.

Eddie did a classic double take: glance, look away, then snap around when he recognized me. He was up and pivoting around me around to get the whole effect.

"Wow! You look fabulous! My god, you're gorgeous."

"Yup, I do clean up well, don't I," as I stepped into his hug. "Wait until you see the Visa bills, though."

"Never mind Visa, sit down, let me look at you. Wow."

Eight

My trip down memory lane ends quickly as a squad car pulls up. I start to shake, thinking the police might have somehow connected me to Mr. Taylor. A beautiful, dark girl—Trinidad, Bahamas, some exotic place—gets out.

"Morning ma'am, how are you today." God, I hate being called ma'am.

"I'm just fine, darling. Did I do something wrong?" I had jay walked a few streets over, but I couldn't see her stopping me for that; that was blocks ago.

"No ma'am. I just saw your cart and all your things on it and wondered if you had a place to stay. I could drive you downtown to a shelter; there's the one on Jasper Avenue and it's real nice."

Right. Where I used to volunteer. I try not to show my fear. No shelters for me, everyone being so kind and saying don't be ashamed and we're just here to see you have a warm place and would you like a shower and if you want to talk we're always here. Nice people, kind people, but filled with pity that just kills you inside. No, I know all about those shelters and I'm not going.

I have to reassure this young woman, get her off my back. So I lie, something that comes easier all the time, even for a person who always claimed honesty was the first virtue in life.

"Isn't that just funny, you thinking I'm a bag lady. Well, I guess I look like one. But the truth is, my apartment building had a small fire last night and I just grabbed what I could while they get the place cleaned up. I'm on my way to stay with a friend for a few days."

Officer Trinidad or Cuba stands, feet apart, hands on her hips. Her bullshit detector is humming; I can almost hear it.

"Where's your friend live? I could drive you there." My mind is whirling. Where, where would my friend live, if I had one? The only location I think of is Gold Bar, where Eddie's house was, and—bonus—it's near the river valley and Capilano Park. I can use the fire pits there and hide out for the night.

"You know that drug store on 101st? Just off Gretzky? It's right by there. If you drop me there, I can pick up my prescription and then it's just a few steps to my friend's." I thought the prescription was genius; how many bag ladies have prescriptions?

My quick response seems to satisfy the young officer. She did wince a bit when I got in the car; I hadn't found a place to clean up in two days.

As we drive across the south side, her remark about the women's shelter spins me back in time.

Once I finished redecorating the house, I mentioned to Eddie that the drug store at Capilano Mall was looking for help and I was going to apply.

My easy-going Eddie could turn in a flash into a very opinionated, stubborn man. And on this point he was mulish: I'd been working all my life, we didn't need extra money, he wanted me home taking care of things, maybe learning some crafts, working on my poetry and making us a nice life.

I fought back. I was independent, didn't need a man to look after me, I'd always made my own way and didn't want to feel useless. I needed to work. I wasn't a pampered Persian cat sitting on a pillow.

We at last settled on volunteer work. Maybe I could work at one of those places that sorted donated clothes for the poor, or a literacy program, something to help people that didn't have it as good as we did.

Within days, I was working at the new women's shelter downtown.

Eddie liked my choice of volunteer position. He sent a hefty check to the foundation and proudly told his friends I was helping out with homeless women. It just drove him crazy, he said, how society could let its own go hungry and without a bed. Sure, some of them brought it on themselves, he said, with drugs and alcohol or what have you. But some had no choice. Like if they were escaping from violence or threat. And in a prosperous city like Edmonton, there was no reason for anyone to sleep on the streets. I wonder what he'd think of my situation now.

My first morning at the shelter, I was shown the rounds by Lillian, a pretty woman with a nice, easygoing manner. She chatted casually with the girls and women staying at the shelter, asked what they'd been up to and what their plans were for the rest of the day.

Gloria was quite a different story. What she was doing working as a care-giver was beyond me. She seemed suspicious and resentful toward the small group that had come in to make tea, and to cover it up, she was cloyingly, overbearingly nice. The three young girls moved their teapot to the far corner of the room, away from the fawning condescension that oozed from every pore of Gloria's body.

I thought I'd do well to emulate Lillian and treat the people there like I'd treat anyone else, people I meet at the bank or while buying groceries or picking up dry cleaning. It seemed to work, and I enjoyed my mornings at the shelter.

Two afternoons a week, I worked at a street kitchen or at a clothing bank if they were short of help. I became acquainted with a number of the caregivers in different agencies and churches.

That time was a real eye opener; I'd never realized there were so many down and out, desperate people in a city enjoying an economic boom. They ranged from very young to very old, completely lucid to clearly lost. Some obviously were victims of addiction; with others, it wasn't as obvious what misfortunes they'd suffered, why they were on the street. A few had jobs, but they didn't make enough to pay the ever-climbing rents in Edmonton those days.

But there was one thing they all had in common: the need to be treated with respect, kindness and empathy. It amazed me, I told Eddie, how they maintained their dignity, living as they did. He knocked on the dining table three times: "There but for the grace of God ..." He was so right.

When Eddie and I left for our trip to Hawaii, I'd been volunteering for more than a year. I told Lillian I would be gone for two weeks, and I'd see her when I got back home. But I never did get back home, or back to my volunteer job.

No, there was no way I would go to a women's shelter. From volunteer to victim? My pride couldn't take that. Imagine running into Gloria. "Well, look at you, poor thing. Did that boy friend of yours throw you out, the rotten jerk? You know what they say about the cow and the milk. Now, you just sit down here and I'll go get a Nice, Warm, Clean bed ready for you. Did you want to have a shower, dear? You do have a bit of an aroma to you, and no point in getting the nice bed dirty."

God, I'd die first.

Nine

We're at the drug store now, and Officer Cuba hands me her card. "Call if you ever need help. I work the south side mostly and I'm usually around here or close by when I'm on shift."

I thank her and sneak into the store, trying to avoid the young sales clerks with their smart clothes, skinny figures and piercings. I just don't get that, all those holes in hideous places. I can hardly talk to someone who has a shiny silver thing bouncing on their lip or stuck through an eyebrow. Guess I'm a bit old fashioned maybe, but what is stylish about maiming yourself?

After two of these skinny little things offer to help me, I figure I better get out of the store. I peer cautiously around the parking lot and, thankfully, Officer Cuba and her police car are gone. I feel pressure on my bladder; it's about 12 blocks to the ravine entrance, if I remember right, so I have to hurry.

I'm glad I was able to fake out the police woman about the shelter. I cannot, will not go to any of those women's shelters. Never.

It's a long trudge from here to Capilano Park. To break up the journey, I wander through the neighbourhoods along the way, lost in memories.

I never applied for another regular job again after the steakhouse. The pretense of acting like I'd just left my home, fresh from the shower and with newly laundered clothes, proved too hard to keep up. It was easier when I had my monthly recreation pass, but then the outdoor pool closed for the season and the only place to clean up was the laundromat on Whyte. But that was never a complete job and depended on no other customers being present at the time.

I got bits of work here and there, like at the car wash when the cashier called in sick, another afternoon's work watering the big planters on the restaurant patio by the rail yards. It was all cash under the table.

I answered an ad for a part time housekeeper. The house was a tiny jewel with an equally tiny occupant. The woman was in her late seventies, perhaps older, and spoke with fluttering hand gestures that reminded me of silk scarves moving in the breeze. She interviewed me for about 10 minutes and decided I would do. It was just her in the house, and she really preferred to do her own cleaning, but the "osteo" was getting bad and she needed help. I started the next day and finished the cleaning job in just under two hours. She seemed pleased, and asked if I could make tea. We chatted for about an hour. She told me about her life: she had been a school librarian, never married, but she had a niece who lived in town and was very close to her. We agreed I'd come back the next week and she handed me an envelope with my pay.

This went on for several weeks. I came to enjoy her company, and she found little extras for me to do—packing some clothes for charities, weeding the tiny front flower bed—and always paid me a bonus for the extra work. I suspect she had guessed my situation and she often pressed food on me, insisting it would only go to waste if I didn't take it.

I bought a couple of outfits at the thrift store with my pay; I always tried to be fresh and tidy when I came to her house.

When I rang the doorbell the last time I went there, I was greeted by a tall, rigid looking woman about my age. She wore her steel grey hair combed back with military preciseness, and her mannerisms matched that military bearing. She was appalled—simply appalled—that her aunt had hired me knowing so little about me and with no references. But she was going to find a cleaner for her aunt, someone reliable, and I was no longer needed. And I was not to come to the house again.

I asked to speak to her aunt, to say goodbye, but was told she was not well and was having a nap.

The woman watched me leave the yard and I managed to hold in my tears until she slammed the door. I glanced back quickly and saw a tiny hand wave at me from the bedroom window.

Afterward, I found less and less work that suited a person of no fixed address. I swept the sidewalk in front of a gift shop for five dollars, broke down cardboard boxes for recycling for three, washed pots at a restaurant for six. I had a full week's worth of work at a bar that was being renovated, peeling beer posters off the wall and chipping old tiles from the washroom walls. It was dirty work but I always cleaned up in the women's room before leaving for the day. The pay at the end of the week was certainly welcome in my damage deposit fund which was growing, but nowhere near what I needed to rent an apartment.

Another thing I noticed around then was that panhandlers no longer stopped me for handouts. I was beginning to look homeless. That was maybe three weeks ago and I know I'm looking shabbier by the day.

Ten

Hardisty Rec Centre is on my right as I walk down 106th. I wish I had the price of admission; a long, hot shower would be great, but I'm at least two dollars short unless I dip into my savings. And it's getting close to sundown. I don't want to be tripping down the slopes into the picnic area in the dark.

Finally, I'm here. Capilano Park is more groomed than Mill Creek ravine; it slopes gently from the residences that surround it down to the river. There are paved trails and picnic sites, and at the east end, a boat launch where we'd met Eddie's friend and gone for a boat ride down the river. It was a great experience to see the city from the water; there was a diversity of development you never noticed up the bank. I was also impressed with what a beautiful treasure the city had in this green river valley.

I know the recreation crews have stopped stocking the log cradles for the season so I pick up broken sticks as I go. I look for an isolated picnic spot with a fire pit, dodging joggers in shoes costing more than all my possessions together. I don't envy them. I just wish I'd been smarter about things.

Finally, I find what I'm looking for: a picnic table sheltered from the park path by shrubs, with a river view. I think how nice, just like that time Eddie and I ate dinner on the patio at the grand old Macdonald Hotel, with the river below us and little white fairy lights in the trees. There are no fairy lights here, but then again there's no huge tab to dine in this "restaurant."

With the fire going, I get out one of my pots. It's in the zipper bag right at the bottom of my cart, so I have to unload everything. The faucet is only a hundred feet up the path but I hesitate at leaving everything I own on a picnic bench. I decide to trust the odds and hurry to get water.

My heart stops when I return and round the bushes hiding my table. There's a girl with long hair hanging around her face, wearing some of the dirtiest, raggiest clothes I've ever seen, and she's going through my things. I yell, and she drops to her knees, holding the bag of vegetable scraps to her chest.

My god, she's almost a baby. I see the tears running down her cheeks, and how her hands shake. She seems to have nothing but the clothes she's wearing and I feel sorry for her. Her face is hollow, her eyes dead looking. I'm thinking drug addict, and I'm scared. Then she gives me a timid smile.

"I'm sorry. I'm sorry. I shouldn't have touched your stuff. I'm just …" Her voice breaks off.

I take the bag from her, roughly, and snap at her. "Go find more sticks for the fire. I'll make us some soup. And wash your hands; there's a tap just up there."

She runs off with disbelief in her eyes, but she's soon back with an armful of wood.

"I'm Cara, lady. I can't believe you're going to give me some of your food. Most people run me off, or throw things at me."

"Well, I'm not most people. Do you happen to have any salt with you?"

"Nope ma'am, I have nothing. But I can go to the houses up there and ask for some."

That ma'am grates on me. "Don't call me ma'am, go find some salt, and be quick. I'm getting real hungry here."

"Me too, ma'am. Oops, I'm sorry lady. I'll be fast."

I use a little water to wash the peelings and carrot ends, then air-chop them, cutting my thumb in the process. Crazy how you never think about cutting boards when you've got them. I had three or four, and I never thought there would be a day I'd miss them more than, well, the mix master or the gas range, even.

Eddie insisted on the stainless steel gas range. He said a good cook needed good tools.

And we did eat well. I picked up some great recipes from the Internet and television. I loved to surprise Eddie with new dishes. We had a coq au vin that Eddie raved about; he said he wanted to have the kids over to try it. The next weekend was his birthday, so we invited them to help celebrate.

The two daughters and the son had long ago quit bringing appetizers and wine, and they always left soon after they'd eaten. For this visit, their dad's birthday, they brought a card and a gift-wrapped box of golf balls. The son pointed out how they were top quality, meaning expensive.

Eddie laughed a bit and said the balls could be gold plated, they still wouldn't improve his game. "Besides, I don't golf much these days. We like to go to farmers' markets on weekends, buy some good food and come home and cook it. Seems like a better use of time; can't eat a bad golf score."

I excused myself to check on dinner. The younger daughter followed me into the kitchen.

"Pretty fancy stove you've got. And all these new clothes. Has Dad got any money left or have you spent it all?"

Her sharp tone made my eyes burn with tears, but I wasn't going to let them spill.

"Don't think you can come waltzing in here and take over. Replace my mother. My dad really loved her, you know. You're just some piece of ass to him, I bet. You won't last long before he gets tired of you."

As calmly as I could, I asked her to get everyone seated and said I'd bring dinner out. I was so relieved when that dinner was over that I didn't even mind that they left their plates at the table and went home.

The older daughter, the one who was more ambivalent toward me, broke up with her boyfriend. Because their shared home was originally his apartment, she wound up with nowhere to go. We put her up for three weeks while she found a new place. She barely acknowledged my presence during her visit; it was all, "Dad, where do you keep the towels; I need a fresh one." Or, "Dad, do you have any chips?" while she hunkered down in my favourite chair in front of the TV. I put a bowl of chips on the end table beside her and her hand reached for them, but she never took her eyes off the screen or said thank you.

She dumped her clothes in the laundry room and I washed them, leaving them clean and folded on her dresser. The clothes were never mentioned.

I made it a habit to be out of the house when Eddie was at work. Apparently she was looking for a job, but how a person could find work by watching television all day was beyond me.

I stopped encouraging Eddie to ask the kids over after that.

Eleven

Cara is back with a little baggie of salt and a middle-aged guy in work clothes. He was from the wastewater treatment plant at the park entrance, he said, and just came back with Cara to see if we were okay. His eyes took in the little pot of soup cooking, and my bags and rolls of bedding.

"It's supposed to be frost tonight. Where are you ladies sleeping?"

The lie slips off my tongue so easily. "Oh we'll probably go over to one of the women's shelters downtown. They're nice and clean, you know."

"Well, that's a long walk. How about a bus ride on me?" He pulls a handful of change out of his pocket—"They only take exact change, you know"—and piles it on the picnic table. Then he adds a 10 from another pocket.

"Well, you ladies take care. You ever get bored, we give plant tours every Wednesday at one o'clock." He whistles his way down the path and out of sight.

I take the salt from Cara and add a bit to the soup. "Okay, this looks ready but I don't have an extra bowl so you'll have to eat from the pot." She's finished her share before I barely get my spoon in, despite talking steadily between slurps.

Her mom is mostly okay, she says, but she got married again last year and the guy is a jerk. At first, it was just, y'know, he always wanted to know where Cara was going and where she'd been. He ragged on her for her school marks, her messy room and put a five minute limit on her phone calls. He was always, like, feeling her mom up in front of her and leering at her.

Her mom was out one night and he walked in drunk, cornering her in her bedroom and clutching at her, slobbering on her face, her breasts. She took off out of the house and went to a girlfriend's, but after a few days, the girl's mom said she had to go. She bummed around all summer, sleeping over at different places with people she met on Whyte, but her options are running out and it's getting too cold to make it on the streets. She's not sure what she'll do next.

I suggest she get in touch with her mom, tell her what happened. She shrugs that off, saying her mom probably would take the guy's side.

With a big yawn, she pulls her hood over her head and slips her in hands inside the too-long sleeves, then lies down on the bench seat. She shudders with cold for a few minutes, then appears to be fast asleep. I cover her with my spare blanket and she snuggles in with little kitty-like snores.

I clean up and add the last of the sticks to the fire. I make tea and add the contents of my salvaged bottle raid. It's not bad, actually, if you don't mind gin, rum, tequila and whiskey together, and it warms me as it slides down.

It's peaceful here, and I enjoyed talking with Cara.

It's been a few days since I've had a real conversation with some-one—lying to Officer Cuba doesn't count as conversation—and I realize I miss the times back at the ravine.

Most afternoons, we'd meet up in the clearing and pool our groceries—bought, begged or "borrowed"—and make a group meal.
My concept of stealing was altering a bit. Let's just say I was getting
complacent and didn't refuse to share others' pilfered goods. I
wound up being the official cook because everyone liked my dinners
best. We would sit while dinner cooked, listening to distant traffic
sounds from Whyte, and talking about whatever came to mind. Just
like normal people sitting on a backyard patio or in a restaurant
lounge.

Hannah wasn't often there, but she was present the night we were
planning a Canada Day celebration.

We all threw out ideas—go to the river valley ball park at Telus
Field to watch fireworks, take the bus to West Edmonton Mall's
indoor water park and have a beach party, chip in to make a really
superb feast—when Luke cried out, "I've got it!"

"Let's go camping!"

His comment didn't register for a moment, then we heard a
high-pitched keening that turned out to be Betty, giggling like a
maniac with her chins and rolls shaking and wobbling. That set us
all off, laughing at the outrageous irony of a group of homeless people going camping. The laughter would just about settle down, then
somebody would take off again, and away we'd all go. The last to
stop was Luke.

Then I realized he wasn't laughing, he was weeping hopelessly. I
touched his shoulder and he threw himself across my lap, shaking
with sobs. I gave him a few tentative pats on the back, feeling my
own tears coming on.

I was surprised when Hannah came over and lifted Luke into a
bear hug.

"He gets like this sometimes. Sometimes it's just too much for
him … missing his little sisters, his dog, wanting to go home."

"Why doesn't he go home then?" I asked.

"His parents threw him out. They—especially big, self-made-businessman dad whose golf cronies are more important than his family—will not have a fag for a son. That's what they said. That he's dead to them. And they're not even Jewish."

The recognition hit me like a hammer. Luke had seemed familiar from day one, like I'd known him, or someone like him, before. Randy. My brother.

The kids at school clued into Randy early in junior high. He was good looking, excelled at sports and was a good scholar. None of that stopped the awful taunts: homo, queer, pansy, bum boy. It was weird how they knew he was different, and of course, difference was unacceptable. Randy left right after graduation, to go to Montreal, where he hoped people's attitudes might be more liberal. I don't know about their attitudes, but his grew steadily worse and he slipped more and more often into the moods he called black holes. He barely made it through university and only with the help of an understanding professor.

I didn't know how serious it was getting and was shocked when his friend called to tell me Randy was dead. He didn't want to say how, but I got it out of him: in the metro one rush hour, he pitched himself off a platform onto the rails in front of hundreds of horrified commuters. The health board scraped up his remains, cremated them and sent Randy home in a small cardboard box. I took it to the cemetery where mom was buried and, vigilant for any workers or officials that might be around, lifted a section of sod and poured the ashes in. I just wish there could be someone to do the same for me when the time comes.

Under the sorrow I felt for my brother's short, sad life, I was relieved Mom had gone first. This would have killed her.

Luke's crying slowed to deep, wracking shudders and Hannah led him away to his clearing. I was quite surprised at her compassion; maybe my first opinion of the girl was too harsh.

She came back quickly, saying Luke was asleep.

"That was really good of you, Hannah. Helping comfort Luke like that."

"Right, well, we're both from Riverbend, so we understand each other. Nothing but perfection allowed in that up-scale snobville." She waved and left for her own place.

I had a cat for a while. A kitten, really. She showed up one night while I was cleaning out my cooler bag. At first she kept her distance, staring at me suspiciously, and I wondered if she was one of the feral cats that were multiplying in the city's ravines and river valley. She didn't have a wild look, though, and when I threw her a piece of cheese, she snatched it up greedily.

I didn't throw the next piece as far, forcing her to come closer. On the third piece, I reached out to grab her, but she was faster than me and scooted off into the shrubbery.

I forgot about her and finished with the cooler, then began to shake out the blankets and things I'd cleaned at the laundromat that day. It had taken every last bit of my change; I'd have to find some work soon.

When I turned to place the blankets on my pallet, I was startled to see the kitten, curled up in a ball, purring on my pillow. I moved her when I lay down to sleep. Five minutes later she was back, snuggled against my neck. I relocated her twice more, then gave up. She was warm and the purring was somehow comforting.

Luke named her Diamond Lil for the diamond-shaped white spot on her forehead. Lilly soon became a camp favourite, though we had to be sure she didn't follow us when we left the ravine. I chased her back three times one morning before she finally gave up.

Mr. Taylor and Luke took charge of finding kitty tidbits for her, always keeping plastic bags in their pockets and politely asking for tidbits at restaurant back doors. The kitten ate almost better than we did, and she soon became a healthy, young adult.

She wasn't waiting for me one evening and I merely assumed she was out mousing or exploring. I didn't see her the next morning, and began to worry. When three days passed, I accepted the inevitable: she was gone. Luke thought she'd wandered up to one of the houses up the hill and decided to stay. Hannah, ever looking to get a rise out of me, suggested coyotes. I didn't care to speculate; I was just heartbroken that another thing I loved had been taken away.

Twelve

My fellow ravine rats, as we'd christened ourselves, went to the downtown farmers market on Saturdays; I went to the one in Old Strathcona where I was less likely to run into anyone from my old life.

Eddie and I, and our circle of friends, were downtown people. We frequently met in Edmonton's arts district where we saw theatre at the Citadel, went to concerts at Winspear Centre, shopped at City Centre and ate at our favourite places like Bistro Praha, Hotel Mac and Ruth's Chris Steak House. When the new fourth street market opened, we all shopped there, then met for coffee and sometimes lunch at one of the new places springing up in a reviving downtown core.

So my choice of market was obvious: the one in the old bus barns on the south side.

Near closing time, the vendors practically gave away produce rather than having to pack it back home. With the small cooler bag I picked up at a garage sale, I could keep things fresh for days.

One Saturday, on impulse, I bought a potted geranium. I dug out some grass and planted it, proud of my flower garden. It was too late to plant tomatoes. I wished I had thought of it earlier, so I could reminisce on Eddie and I tending our plants, anticipating the luscious crop we'd usually eat before it made it to the kitchen. I still missed Eddie with a burn that sometimes took me to bed to cry until I was asleep.

That same week, I found a camouflage print tarp at a garage sale for a dollar. When it was hanging around my space, I felt more secure. It's amazing how little things become precious when you've lost everything.

Of course, it was "summertime," and "the livin' was easy." I didn't let myself think about what I would do when it started to get colder, when winter came.

Betty came home one day with a newspaper article about some homeless people living in a place the media called "Tent Town." It was somewhere on the north side in a huge field where a meat packing plant had been.

We decided to go on a group excursion to see how these people were managing. Maybe we could pick up some tips. Luke offered to research bus routes and panhandle enough change for our bus fare. We decided the next Friday would be a good time for the trip. Betty knew a garden where the beets were getting to be a good size; she'd make borscht as a gift to our hosts and hostesses.

I couldn't beg. I would rather go hungry than ask for money. A few times, people had silently handed me coins or a bill, usually when I was sweeping walks or doing some other under-the-table job. But ask for money? That would never happen.

Mr. Taylor and I were frequent visitors at the Old Strathcona Library. Both of us had cards; mine was paid in full from the time before—that was how I thought of my old life compared to the current one—whereas Mr. Taylor had accepted a free card based on living below the government's low income cut-off line. The library was a nice place to pass the time and I would often look up things for

Betty on the Internet. She had a great interest in the use of herbs as medicine and Wicca theory. She would never come with me; I had an idea that perhaps she was persona non grata over some incidence in the past.

Frequently, we sat at the same table as a young woman, a student maybe. She and Mr. Taylor spoke to one another but I had never exchanged a word with her.

I was immersed in Gardening for Dummies one morning when I sensed a presence beside me. The young woman.

"Excuse me. I'd like to talk to you please. Could I buy lunch for you if you have time?"

I was suspicious right off, but she seemed nice and lunch was lunch. We introduced ourselves and she suggested a small café just up Whyte.

Once settled with soup and a sandwich at an outdoor table, she began to talk.

"What I wanted to talk to you about, well, I was wondering if you would tell me about being homeless? Like how you cope with things like laundry, showers and baths, things like that?"

My defenses kicked immediately.

"What makes you think I'm homeless?" I barked.

She jerked back in her chair with a frightened look.

"Well, you're always with Mr. Taylor, and you have a cart like his with all your stuff on it."

"Why do you want to know things like that anyhow?" I asked. She lowered her head a bit as her cheeks flushed.

"Well, I'm a writer. I write stories for magazines. I asked my editor about doing a story on homeless people, kind of a day in the life of a street person. Y'know?"

"If you want to know what's it's like to be a street person, leave your wallet at home and come hang out with me for a week or two.

Then you'll know what to say in your story." She could see I was getting angry.

"No, I couldn't do that. I have, like, responsibilities at home."

"And are you going to get paid for this story?"

"Of course. It's how I make my living."

"Well, just suppose *I* write a story about living on the street and *I* get paid for it. Why should *you* make money off *my* story? Think up your own damn stories!" Several people were watching us now; I was getting louder with each word. I pushed my chair away from the table and got ready to rise.

"I'm sorry, please. I didn't mean to offend you." She reached across the table to touch my hand. I looked down: she was holding out several 20s.

I plunked back in my chair. "I write, you know. I write poetry."

"I'd love to read some of it, if you'd let me. But please, take the money. For wasting your time. Insulting you."

I considered for a moment then put the bills in my pocket.

"Don't waste your money using the washers at the laundromat. Wash and rinse things in the big sinks at the back, wring them hard, and save your change for the dryer. Watch for dryers with time left over. Go to garage sales. When the people are getting ready to shut down, they'll give you things for next to nothing. Some of those things, you can get a few dollars for at a pawn shop." I talked in between finishing my meal while she hastily wrote notes.

"What is the hardest thing about living on the street?" she asked.

I thought for a moment. There were a lot of things that bothered me, but the worst one? Finally, it came to me.

"People thinking you're dirty or stupid or dangerous just because you don't have a home. Treating you like a lower form of life."

"Oh!" She seemed surprised at this. "I never thought about that. But I guess it's true. People are suspicious and wary of anyone … different from themselves."

"Right. And those looks of pity. I want to yell at them. 'I used to be just like you. I didn't choose this kind of life. And what happened to me could happen to you too. So don't act so smug when you throw a quarter my way.'"

"I see what you mean. 'There but for the grace of God ...'" Yes, just like Eddie had said.

What was worse, I wondered afterward? Begging or prostitution? I'd just sold myself for 60 dollars. Maybe panhandling wasn't so shameful after all.

Thirteen

The day came for our visit to Tent Town. It took two hours and three buses to get to the location in the paper, then we couldn't see anything. Just a big field. Luke noticed, then, that it was hilly at the front of the plot, and maybe the camp was behind the rise. We trudged across the weeds and dust until we saw it: a handful of makeshift shacks and tents scattered amid a grove of trees.

There was a woman sitting in front of one, tending a small cooking fire. She looked up and smiled a welcome. Soon we were sitting around her fire, explaining the reason for our visit. She told us about being burned out of her rental home. Afterward, she wasn't able to find another apartment. Vacancy rates are at an all-time low and most places want a three-month damage deposit. Her boyfriend got back from Fort McMurray to find her squatting in a friend's unheated garage. He heard about this community and decided they'd be better off here. The shelters downtown don't accept couples and they wanted to be together.

The boyfriend arrived about then and Betty brought out her offering of borscht. Pots and bowls materialized, the soup was heated, shared and declared "divine nectar." Funny about borscht, you either love it or hate; there is no ambivalence.

Mr. Taylor went off to see if someone living further out was an old friend.

Luke and I volunteered to accompany the woman to get water for dishes. Down the other side of the hill was a service station that let them fill water containers once a day. It took us a while to fill and carry the vessels back.

We got there to find a sight that appalled Luke and me: Betty and the boyfriend were sitting with a bottle of rye between them. Betty's face was getting flushed already, a sign Mr. Taylor says means trouble.

Mr. Taylor showed up just then, taking in the situation in a flash. We gathered our things quickly and called Betty to come with us. She said she wasn't coming.

Mr. Taylor tried to talk to her, but she kept shaking her head. Then he talked to the boyfriend, maybe suggesting he put the bottle away. Finally he shrugged and came back to where we were waiting.

"Shall we be off?" I looked back over my shoulder. Betty was laughing and slapping her thighs. The party was heating up.

"We're not leaving her here, are we?" I was worried about her, having never seen her drunk yet.

"She is a grown woman with a free will," Mr. Taylor intoned. "I am not her keeper, nor can I pry her away when a bottle is in front of her." I looked back once more, then ran to catch up with them.

Betty came home four days later, nonchalant as if she'd just been up the avenue to buy a newspaper. She came bearing gifts: a leather-bound classic for Mr. Taylor, a beautiful notebook for my poetry and a set of replacement wheels for Luke's out-of-commission skateboard. Luke whooped and took off to repair his board. Mr. Taylor and I exchanged a glance and went to our separate areas.

Fourteen

I'm remembering mostly the good parts now, not the horror and hopelessness of my situation.

There were some nights I cried until I was choking, muffling the sobs with the lion's head blanket.

There were days when I sat on benches watching the river, gut-wracked with grief, not caring to look for work or bottles or restaurant leavings, or if I lived or died.

Other days, I was filled with white hot rage that fate had thrown this my way. I wanted to track down Eddie's kids and do them physical harm.

Rainy days brought me so low I'd think about death, and how to achieve it. I'd lost everyone I'd loved and I couldn't see the point of going on.

Once, I really did contemplate ending it. Air One, the police helicopter, was circling the ravine that night and I suddenly found myself sitting in the middle of the helicopter's spotlight. In the cockpit light, I could see the pilot and passenger peering down at me and laughing. I don't know what they were saying, but I suddenly felt so pitiful that I had my sharp knife out and was staring at my wrists.

But I couldn't do it. It was not so much the pain but the thought of Mr. Taylor or Betty finding me, or worse yet, Luke. I couldn't do that to my friends.

The fire is down to small coals now and I'm sleepy. I wrap up in my lion cover, slide under the picnic table and go to sleep.

The cold wakes me early the next morning. I haul myself out from under the table—not anywhere near as luxurious as my "loft"—and pack everything away. Amazingly, Cara is still sleeping on the bench, on her back now and snoring lightly. I think about taking my blanket back, but she obviously can use it, and I really don't want to wake her. She seems like a good kid, but I don't need a hanger-onner. It's going to be enough trouble taking care of myself. I tuck the water plant guy's tenner under the blanket by her chin and leave quietly.

The park washroom facility is locked, so I head off to the mall to get warm and cleaned up.

Eddie and I called it Carpal Tunnel Mall. It had the same number of syllables as the mall's real name and suited the mall's personality. Can a mall have a personality? Why not, if colours have smells?

The name came to us when we were getting some food from Edo, the Japanese fast food outlet, before going for groceries. We found a table in the food court beside two retirees carping about rising property taxes and living on a fixed income. One of them started to complain about his wrist; his doctor diagnosed carpal tunnel syndrome and suggested he reduce his time on e-mail and surfing the Internet. Eddie and I couldn't look at each other: fixed income and computers? It was just too hilarious. Like, give us a break.

It's getting colder by the minute and it's raining now. I'm shivering so hard it's all I can do to pull my cart behind me. One wheel is loose and I have no tools to fix it, so my progress is slow.

I stop at a few bus shelters along the way to get out of the rain, now turning icy and sharp. There's a paper box in one. The headline reads: "Senior found dead in ravine." Sub-head: "Apparently homeless male beaten to death and robbed, say city cops." There is a stark photo of police and emergency workers standing in a clearing, looking much as I had last seen it, with a tarp-covered lump in the background. I still have the water guy's change and could buy the paper, but somehow I don't want to read it. I've accepted Mr. Taylor's death; why re-open old wounds?

My mind goes round and round in circles. If I could get cleaned up, I could look for a job and find a cheap place to stay. If I had a place to stay, I could stay cleaned up and keep a job. If I had a job … and so on and so on. Now I know what my mom meant when she talked about vicious circles. I feel like I'm on a merry-go-round and I can't get off.

I hear yells and shouting behind me, then I'm shoved and knocked to the ground. A group of students rush by me, jeering and kicking my cart over. The fear and the shock make me let go, and as I stagger to my feet, they are pointing and shouting. "Crazy old alky! Peed herself! Gonna poop too, you old bag?" They stumble off, doubled over and cawing that they'd scared, "That old bum all right!"

One turns to yell at me, "Stinking old loser. Go lie down in the street and get run over! You smell up our neighbourhood."

And I do feel like lying down in the street. What else is there to do? I haven't washed in days, now my clothes are wet and reeking. Why not just run in front of a truck?

I'm drained of energy, and my legs are aching cold and chafed from the wet jogging pants. I scramble to pick up my things and reload the cart.

Fifteen

The scene at Eddie's front door when I got back from my trip to Saskatchewan plays over and over in my head.

"Get your lazy ass off this property and don't come back. And if you try and find our dad, we'll have you arrested." The younger daughter was doing the yelling; the older one was wiping tears from her eyes and clutching her sister's arm. The son stood beside me, hanging his head in apology.

We'd been living together for just over two years when Eddie suggested a trip to celebrate our "anniversary." He wanted to go to Hawaii and maybe even think about doing "the dirty deed"—get married—while we were there. I don't know why I balked at making our relationship legal, I just did. Eddie gave in gracefully, saying at least he was going to move some things around when we got back to make sure I was set up if anything happened to him.

The trip was a dream. We ran into two couples Eddie knew through work and we partied with them the whole two weeks. They were fun, and funny, and we laughed as much as we ate and drank. Eddie and I were in paradise, and it wasn't just because we were in Hawaii.

The night before we had to go home, Eddie was on the lanai and I was packing our suitcases. I heard a thump and ran out to see what happened.

Eddie was struggling to sit up. He said he just starting feeling dizzy a bit, and next thing he was on the lanai floor. I made him come in to lie down and he seemed fine, so we put it down to too much fun, and he'd see a doctor when we got home.

Back in Edmonton, there was a phone message for me. My uncle Harold—my Mom's brother—had died, and his lawyer had called. Harold's landlord wanted someone to take care of his things so they could re-let his suite.

Eddie arranged the flights for me, gave me a handful of travellers' cheques and off I went. Since my return flight was in the early afternoon while Eddie was at work, I said I'd take a cab from the airport and be there when he got home.

It was surprising how little time it took to clear up my uncle's life. Never married and with few possessions other than his clothes, I locked the door of his suite and gave the keys to the landlady, telling her she could keep his television for the next renter. Using the power of attorney document I found in his night table drawer, I cashed his last pay cheque and counted the money I had. Three hundred in cash—Harold was paid weekly by the warehouse where he worked part time—and about two hundred in travellers' cheques. It seemed quite a rich sum at the time.

Next I went to the storage centre where I had packed away my things and arranged to have about five boxes sent to Edmonton. The rest I sold to the storage centre manager for a hundred dollars. There wasn't all that much, really: a couch, a chair, a dinette and a bed with a matching dresser. I really had lived a sparse live style, I now realized.

I arranged with the bank to deposit my savings and RRSPs into Eddie's and my joint account and that was it—I was finished with small town Saskatchewan.

I stop for a rest at a bus shelter just as a bus grinds away in a cloud of exhaust. An off-boarding passenger looks at me with disgust and says to her companion, "It was bad enough when these bums were all over downtown. Now there's so many of them, they're over here ruining our neighbourhoods. Picking through our garbage. You just can't go anywhere any more without running into these filthy street people! Why doesn't someone for god's sake do something?"

Right, why doesn't someone for god's sake do something?

The mall is a comfort after the chilly walk. A quick scan tells me no one is paying attention to me, so I head down the corridor to an out-of-the-way washroom. Guess it isn't so out-of-the-way after all. Two girls wearing nametags from the discount clothing store are sitting on the sinks sharing a cigarette, right under the no smoking sign. Their eyes pop open when they see me, then a quick look tells them they are safe. Would a bag lady report them? Who would believe her anyhow?

They both jump off the sinks and stride past me. One lets out a, "Phew," under her breath. I don't blame her.

Working fast, I take out fresh clothes and change, then fill the sink with warm water to soak my dirty pants. I pour in a few soap flakes; I'm running low. I wash as best I can with paper towels and the dispenser soap. I'd love to shampoo my hair, but it's too cold outside. Thinking about the weather, I put on two pairs of pants and double up my socks. A cleaning woman comes in and sees the fear in my eyes. "Nod my bissniss," she murmurs and goes about hers. I finish before her and go back to mall, feeling somewhat normal again.

The thought of the library beckons me. It has a nice natural gas fireplace and lots of magazines. People tend to keep to themselves there. It's as if once they notice or pay attention to you, they're somehow responsible for doing something. Most of the people I run into seem sheepishly relieved that I pass them without asking for money. You can tell they're not bad people; they just don't want to take responsibility. As if they're embarrassed by their good fortune and any contact with someone like me will rub off on them. Like being homeless is a germ or cootie. I guess I used to feel that way myself.

I browse through the stacks for a long time, looking for books I've read before. I want something comforting, something from my past when I could spend an hour reading in the bath tub before crawling into a warm bed. I find two I want and hand them and my card to the library clerk. She scans the card and peers at her computer screen for what seems a lot longer than usual. I notice her glance at me before silently motioning to the library supervisor. The quick, whispered conversation between them makes me want to get out fast; my new sixth sense for trouble tells me something is wrong.

Then the supervisor is beside me, quietly saying my card is expired but they can renew it for no charge, if I would just step over to the counter and fill out a form and …

I just grab my cart and run out, heading for the stairwell. The elevator is too slow. I can hear her calling, "Ma'am, please ma'am, just wait ma'am …" I'm sobbing by the time I hit the main floor. One of the last signs that I belonged to "normal" society had just been taken from me.

I had, for months, managed to keep up the appearance of just any other person out and about, but now I carry the essence of poverty with me. My cart and bags are shabby and dirty; my clothes are mostly clean but have had no acquaintance with an iron; the lack of makeup and face cream, haircuts and manicured nails marks me as a person without means. I looked uncared for, which I am. And now, having lost the few friends I had, I probably have that shifty look of mistrust and an expectation of being told to leave I'd seen on so many others' faces. In short, I now looked what I am—a bum, a person with nowhere to go.

Sometimes finding a place to spend the day is as bad as looking for shelter at night.

I haven't eaten yet today and I'm dying for a coffee. I purchase one from one of the cheap little lunch counters that serves swill, but I'm not exactly in the gourmet beans income category. I load it with four sugars and creams while the server gives me dirty looks.

I sit at one of the plastic tables and reach into my large bag for my notebook. I can't feel it, so I take out each item, one by one. It's not there. Where did it go?

I remember one of the brats who knocked me down swooping to reach for something before he ran off. My notebook? I don't know, but it's definitely gone. One more thing I've lost when I have so little to lose.

The coffee isn't half bad loaded up with cream and sugar. I sip it slowly and submerge myself in memories.

Mostly, I kept returning to the day I returned from looking after my uncle's estate. The cab ride from the airport had been long and I was looking forward to getting home, having a nice bath and waiting for Eddie to get off work.

Sixteen

The cab stopped in front of Eddie's and I got out to pay the driver. I saw Eddie's son coming toward me, wearing a grim expression. My heart started pounding.

"It's Dad. He had a stroke last night."

"Oh my god." My purse dropped to the road and I grabbed his arm desperately. "How is he? Is he all right? How bad was it?"

"Bad." He looked down and shuffled his feet, then turned to go.

"Wait," I yelled at him. "Don't go," I yelled at the driver. I grabbed the son by the arm. "What hospital is he in? I have to go see him."

That's when the younger daughter came out and spat those hateful words at me. "You won't find him, you slut, so don't bother trying!"

I was wild, off my head. I jumped back in the cab and directed the driver to the closest hospital. At the desk, I was told there was no Edward Weston on their patient list. The cab was still waiting outside, so we drove to the west end hospital. There I got the same answer. And the same one at the Grey Nuns and the University. It didn't occur to me to just phone, and by the time I ran out of hospitals, I was down ninety-four dollars and still hadn't found Eddie.

I sunk into the back seat again. I noticed the meter wasn't running and the driver's eyes were sympathetic in the rear view mirror, but I knew he was also itching to get on with his night.

"Where to now, lady?"

I asked him to drive down Whyte to that new hotel. I couldn't remember the name.

I had no idea what to do. Stake out hospital lobbies in case one of Eddie's kids came by to visit him? Sneak into every ICU to see if I could find him? There didn't seem to be an answer.

The hotel rate—$150 per night, plus tax—staggered me. At this rate, I'd be out of money soon. My brain couldn't take any more stress all of a sudden and I made my way upstairs. I slid down the closed door to the carpet and the sobs started. Big, dry heaving sobs shook my whole body. I moaned Eddie's name over and over. My Eddie. My god. My Eddie.

What if he died and I never saw him again? What if he got better and his kids lied about me, kept him from looking for me?

I was out of my mind with worry. The next morning, I hurried down to the lobby for a newspaper, ripping it open to the obituary section. Nothing. Thank god.

I changed some bills and hit the nearest pay phone, calling every hospital I'd visited the night before. Still no record of Eddie. I was going nuts, trying to remember anything—his doctor's name, what clinic he went to—that would help me find him. I was so humiliated by the scene at the house yesterday, I didn't want to call any of his friends to see what they knew. I spent most of the day just walking up and down Whyte, trying to figure out what I could do. I returned to the hotel exhausted, determined to go to sleep. But my fear for Eddie and the rudeness of his kids brought on tears that lasted hours.

I was angry, sorrowful, defeated, in turn or all at one time. It was late before exhaustion let me slip in a restless sleep.

The next morning, after trying to disguise the ravages of my night-long tears, I returned by cab to the house. I wasn't going to be pushed around by those kids; it was my home. I'd lived there with Eddie for more than two years. Surely they wouldn't be so cruel and hateful to deprive me of my only place to stay? They could at least let me get some clothes.

Obviously, I had misjudged their spitefulness. My key wouldn't open the door; they had changed the locks overnight. I banged on the door in frustration. Suddenly, it flung open and Eddie's younger daughter stood glaring at me.

"I thought we told you not to come back here," she hollered. "Go away."

"No. This is my home. My clothes and things are here. Get out of my way." I grabbed her arm to shove her aside, but she wouldn't budge.

"Get out of my way right now or you're going to get clobbered with my bag." I held it aloft, threateningly. With a quick movement, she grabbed the bag from my hand and threw it down the stairs.

I glanced back to check the bag's fate and she took the opportunity to close the door. I shoved back, putting my whole weight into pushing it open, but she gave it a final thrust and I heard the deadlock engage. I continued to pound and holler uselessly until my hands were aching.

Out of the corner of my eye, I saw a police cruiser pull up and saw Mrs. Diotka, the old lady from next door, come out on her front porch. She'd always been friendly; she'd stand up for me.

"What seems to be the problem here?" asked the police officer strolling up the sidewalk.

"It's that girl—Eddie's daughter—she won't let me in the house. I live here with her father."

The officer looked at the closed door, at my bag and its contents on the ground.

"Mrs. Diotka, you know me. You know I live here with Eddie. Tell this police officer it's my house."

The woman had her hands rolled inside her apron and a disapproving glare on her face.

"The kits say you gone; say you steal money from fadder and leaf him."

"That's not true!" I turned back to the officer. "Can't you make her open the door? I live here."

"Ma'am, you got a complaint, come down to the station and fill out a form. We'll look into it and get back to you." He bent down, picked up my bag and handed it to me.

"But right now, you're disturbing the neighbours and you need to leave. I'll cruise by here in a few minutes to make sure you're not still making trouble."

As he climbed back into his cruiser, I heard Mrs. Diotka mutter before she returned to her house, "Maybe you shoudda gat married before liff in his house." And her door banged shut too.

Things were not looking up. And I still hadn't found Eddie. I returned to the hotel and phoned the hospitals again. No luck; no one had a patient of that name. I even called a few private nursing homes but none of them would tell me anything; the protection of privacy act, they said.

I spent the night dreaming up scenarios in which Eddie would wake up and ask to see me and the kids would back down and let me come to him. Or he'd be calling my name, getting himself all worked up and the medical staff would tell the kids to find me—it was a matter of life and death. That the more agitated he became, the lower his chances for survival.

Or even that his son, who never seemed to resent me as much as the two girls, would relent and realize his dad loved me and I should be with him. But he—and everyone else—had no idea where I was, so the scenarios made no sense.

It was another night of fitful dreams and poor sleep.

The next morning, I picked up a newspaper lying on the lobby coffee table and turned to the obituaries. The notice on page B6 of the paper hit me like a truck: "Weston, Edward John. With deep sorrow, we announce the sudden passing of our father, Eddie, at 56 years of age. Survived by his loving children … A private service will be held for family and friends. Donations to your favourite charity in lieu of flowers."

John. I didn't know his middle name was John. I didn't know his brother died before him, and that Eddie and his wife lost a little boy at three years.

I hoped they hadn't cremated him. He talked a couple of times about being buried in a sunny spot, preferably on a hill so he could enjoy the scenery below. He liked the old Pleasant View Cemetery, but it was almost full and a very sought-after location. "People are dying to get in there." Another of Eddie's corny jokes.

So they saved themselves the cost of a funeral, the jerks. And look at the size of the obituary. Cheap little bastards; barely half an inch of type for their dad who would—and did—do anything for them. The paper blurred in front of me and a rushing sound built in my head …

I don't know how much later, the desk clerk and the security guard were leaning over me, their voices sounding far away and echo-y.

"You all right, ma'am?" Damn, that ma'am again. "We think you fainted; you just went down so fast we couldn't catch you." He helped me to my feet and handed me my purse. "You just go up to your room and have a rest maybe. If you need anything, call the front desk."

If I need anything. I wanted to scream at him, "Yeah, I need a home, some money and I need my Eddie." I returned to the room and howled for hours. I wept for Eddie and I wept for myself.

Seventeen

A hand sweeps in front of me and throws my empty coffee cup into a rolling trash can. I look into hostile eyes and know I've overstayed my welcome.

"Mall's closing. Gotta leave now," a harsh voice commands me. Obediently, I get up and walk to the outside doors.

The temperature really dropped while I was in the mall and the snowfall is thick and heavy. The wheels on my cart quickly get bunged up and I stop to clear them. I need to find some shelter for the night.

The snow muffles sound and the parking lot is dead quiet.

I miss my "loft" in the ravine, but I'm afraid to go back there.

I'm more used to the layout around Whyte; there are a number of places around there I could hide out. This is a familiar area, but that was when I had a car, a credit card, a shopping list, a life, a home. I had never viewed this neighbourhood through the eyes of someone with no place to go.

The phone woke me the morning after I'd seen the obituary. Who could be calling? No one knew where I was.

It was hotel reception, asking me to come down; something about verifying my credit card. The girl at the desk was very discreet, beckoning me around the corner. She explained that, when she punched in my daily charges this morning, my credit card came back invalid. I was speechless for a moment, then said I would pay cash. She told me I would have to pay for that night's stay as well unless I was checking out by noon. My money was going fast.

Next, I went to the instant teller by the front doors and entered my pass word. I watched in horror as the machine sucked in the card and a message appeared: "Invalid PIN number. Please contact your branch bank immediately."

The reality of it sunk in. Eddie's kids had cancelled the credit and bank cards. The nearest branch of my bank was about six blocks away. I had to get there and make sure my money was safe. All my funds were in our joint account; surely the kids couldn't close that without my permission.

Half an hour later, I was in tears as the bank manager told me all Eddie's assets, including our joint account, were frozen until the will was probated. This was provincial law and there was nothing she could do about it. She advised I call my lawyer to determine who might be Eddie's executor; perhaps some advance funds could be released to me in the meantime.

Hopelessness broke over me in waves; I knew Eddie hadn't changed his will yet. Why oh why was I so gullible? I should have insisted everything was spelled out for my own protection, but I just blindly assumed nothing would happen, nothing would change. I had just drifted through time, the same way I had all my life, letting the wind set my direction more than my own good sense.

I'd always prided myself on my independence, but it had felt so good to let Eddie take over and let myself be taken care of. Except as it turned out I wasn't.

I took the tissues the bank manager handed me and stumbled outside.

People jostled and shoved me as I stood, in the middle of the sidewalk, realizing I was in extremely dire straights. One thing was certain—I couldn't afford to stay at the hotel past that night, but where could I go?

The bank manager was right. I needed to talk to my lawyer. But where would I find a lawyer who'd take my case for the few dollars I still had left. I'd be lucky if some cheap outfit like Somebody, Someone and Whoever Inc., Ambulance Chasers, would even let me in their office. Was I screwed or what?

Eighteen

My running shoes are soaked from the sleet this afternoon and after a few minutes outside, I can't feel my feet.

I never wore running shoes once I was past school age. They gave me the creeps, so clunky and wide and graceless. I was happy enough when I found these however. The first popped up on Scona Road one night—why was there always just one shoe? A few days later, I found another behind a deli on Whyte and, glory be, it was for the opposite foot. One was a size larger than I usually wore, so I just put on double socks. The shoes looked similar enough to each other that you hardly figured them for mismatched pair. Crazy, huh? There was a day when nothing but good leather touched my feet and here I was, over the moon because I'd found two running shoes that almost matched.

The gas station at the far end of the mall is about to close when I get there, the attendant on her way to the sink to empty the coffee pot. I dash in and beg her to let me have it instead. She looks me over carefully, apparently decides I'm not dangerous and pours the coffee into a cardboard cup. She keeps her eye on me while I add cream and sugar, fasten on a lid.

"No place to stay, lady?" I jerk around at her question. I shake my head, staring at my feet.

"See that house way across there? The white one with the fancy porch rails? The old man who lives there never closes the padlock on his shed. I know that because my boyfriend and I used to sneak in to ... uh, make out. It's dry and if you're quiet, no one will notice you."

I want to kiss her. "Thank you, thank you so much. You don't know how cold I am. It's brutal out there tonight."

"Well, you just hurry over and get some sleep. The old guy wakes up early so be sure you're gone first thing in the morning."

"Thank you. You're a very nice girl. It's pretty late. Is someone coming to pick you up?"

"Oh yeah; my boyfriend will be here any minute. He's got a car now, so we don't need the shed anymore." She laughs and, on impulse, throws some chocolate bars and those things they call Hoo-Hoos, or something, into a bag and hands it to me.

"You're not going to get in trouble for this are you?"

"Whatever. Do you know the profits this oil company posted last quarter? I know that kind of stuff because my boyfriend wants to be a stockbroker. And if they fire me, well Timmy's is paying a dollar an hour more."

I thank her several more times and stand under the gas pump canopy sipping my coffee. It's old and bitter, but it's hot and makes me stop shaking.

A red car pulls up, low to the ground with bluesy music pouring out. The girl slams the gas station door and slides in the front seat. She gives me a cheerful wave as they speed off.

My mind flees to the past again. Eddie had a fine car, all bright chrome and leather seats. He wanted me to learn to drive it, but I'd never driven stick before. After I stalled it five times in half a block, he gave up, saying a lady like me deserved to be chauffeured around anyhow. I loved that car, and the way Eddie would zoom it around the curves in the river valley, the motor humming like a giant cat. We drove to Vancouver in it once, stopping at every fruit stand and souvenir shop we passed. Pretty soon the small storage place behind my head rest was overflowing. We stopped beside two down-and-out looking kids, a boy and a girl, sitting at a roadside picnic table.

I took all the fruit and vegetables we had and piled them on their table. The girl was shy and wouldn't look at me, but her friend was all over Eddie and the car.

"Wow, man, that's a hot number! Miata, is it? Jeez, I'd cut off my right nut for a car like that." Eddie just laughed and told him to keep his nuts; the car cost a bundle and he'd never get one sitting by the highway.

The young man was instantly on the defensive, chin thrust out and fists balled. "You got any idea how hard it is to get work in this town? Yeah, see those plates; you're from Alberta, and everything is booming there. This valley and all around it is in a depression. You try and find a fucking job around here, you fat ass."

Eddie motioned to me to get in the car and we drove away.

"You know, I guess we've got it pretty lucky. Damned lucky in fact." He geared up for the hill, and smiled at me. "Of course, I'm luckier than most. I've got you."

Oh Eddie. God I loved that man.

The girl was right; the shed is unlocked. I slip in and close the door, then feel my way around. Tools hang on one wall and I bump a rake or something. It sounds like a bomb going off and I hold my breath, waiting to be caught. After a few minutes, it seems no one is coming to investigate, so I resume my search.

The far corner has a pile of boxes, and empty flower pots stacked along side. I try the other wall, and the floor beneath it. It's clear and dry and I sit down in relief. It isn't very warm, but at least it keeps the snow and wind out. I wrap in my lion blanket, put my head on my knees and listen to the wind whistling around the shed. I think about the storm when I got sick and Betty got drunk.

Nineteen

It was raining and had been for three days. And it was cold. I spent most of the time huddled under my tarp, wrapped in blankets and trying to read a paperback. The pages were starting to stick together from humidity and the story—one of those where the characters tripped from sunny Greece to sunnier St. Morez, spending impossible sums of money and drinking enough champagne to kill an elephant's liver—was boringly trite and formulaic. I wanted to go to the library, but it was so wet and miserable, I couldn't face the journey.

I fell asleep at some point. It was dark when I awoke, and I needed to go to the bathroom badly.

Coming back from the grove of trees I'd used, I took a wrong turn or something and wound up in a heavily treed area with fallen logs and prickly underbrush. I had no idea where I was going and couldn't see more than two feet ahead of me. I was getting hot from thrashing through the bush. My chest ached from exertion. I have no idea how long I wandered, but finally sat on a stump and cried. I couldn't do this anymore. I wish I had pills, or a razor, but it was all back at my camp.

Then, over my sobs, I heard my name being called. It was Luke. He found me and led me back to my loft. I had been less than a hundred yards away, but the deep bush had disoriented me. Luckily, Luke had been coming home and heard me crying.

I crawled into my shelter and dropped off in exhaustion.

Some time later, I came out of a groggy sleep to the sound of worried voices. I could hear Betty and Mr. Taylor. Betty pulled aside the tarp and helped me to my feet.

"Come on girl. You are sick, you have a fever. We have to get you somewhere warm."

"No, not a shelter. I won't go to a shelter." Even in my delirious state, I was adamant on that point.

"No, not a shelter, dear. We're taking you to my tent to get you dry and warm." With one of them on either side of me, we made it to Betty's clearing. She helped me inside and pulled off my soggy clothes.

"Put these on. They'll warm you up." "They" were a huge flannel nightgown and a pair of heavy cotton socks. She helped me lie down on a small cot opposite her larger bed, and heaped covers and blankets on me. I later found out Luke had gone to the men's hostel downtown and begged the blankets for a "sick friend." They had wanted to come back with him and see if I needed medical aid, but he managed to convince them otherwise.

Betty stayed with me night and day, waking me up to take a few sips of a thick, gruelly soup or to drink some juice. I heard the others—even Hannah—come by periodically to see how I was doing. But mostly I slept.

My fever finally broke on the second night and I awoke the next afternoon to sunshine and a warm breeze. Betty was hanging my blankets and clothes on a rope strung between two trees and I could smell something delicious cooking. I stretched in the warm sun and, looking down at myself, burst out laughing.

Betty turned to me and started laughing as well. The nightgown was monstrous on me—I was down to a size eight from a 10, and Betty was size XXXX—and the socks sagged around my ankles. I could feel my hair standing straight up.

"Well, you're a sight, but you look better than you have in days," she said. "Here, sit. Hannah raided her parents' freezer while they were out last night and we're having beef bourguignon, courtesy of her dad's wine cellar."

What I didn't know was only a splash of the wine went into the cooking pot; Betty was drinking the rest out of a coffee cup.

The others had joined us by this time, each bringing their own bowl and utensils, and a merry supper it was indeed.

Mr. Taylor was the first to notice. "Betty, have you been drinking?"

"None of your business, you little peckerhead. What are the rest of you staring at? Go on, get outta here, this is my place! Get!"

Everyone scrambled away quickly, leaving me with a Betty I'd never seen before. Muttering to herself, calling out occasional obscenities to those rushing away, she threw the rest of the stew into the fire and heaved the pot into the bushes.

"What are you staring at? Think you're pretty special, hey? Those stories about your precious Eddie. Bunch of lies, I bet. Why else didn't you fight to get your house back from those kids?"

I couldn't believe the change in her. She advanced on me with a raised hand. "Get out. You're useless, can't even stand up to a bunch of kids. Dumb bitch; you think anyone believes you? You're just taking advantage of me like everyone else. Go."

I did, running back to the safety of my clearing. All my blankets were still at Betty's but I wasn't going back for them.

Twenty

After the scene at the bank, I called Bob Franks—he was Eddie's lawyer and good friend.

"May I tell Mr. Franks who's calling?" I identified myself. There was a long pause.

"I'm sorry, Mr. Franks won't be able to take your call."

"But I have to talk to him! I need his help. Can I come to the office?"

"I'm afraid not. Mr. Franks will be out for the rest of the day."

I was in a panic, and probably yelling by this time. "I have to see him. He doesn't know what's happened. They've got everything and I don't know where Eddie is and …"

I heard a man's voice come on the line and ask what the problem was.

"Bob. Bob, it's me. Eddie died, did you know? Now the kids have cut off the phone and the credit cards and …"

"Listen. I shouldn't even be speaking to you. The family has taken out a restraining order against you. The kids said you were violent and threatening when you showed up at the house."

I gasped. "No, they yelled at me. Wouldn't let me in the house. I have nothing. You need to help me."

"I can't help. You have no rights in this situation. You'd best just pack up and go back where you came from."

"But wait. We lived common law for over two years. Doesn't that mean I'm entitled to something? Anything?"

"In some cases it would, if, for example, Eddie had died intestate. But there is a will that clearly spells out the distribution of his estate, and you're not in it."

"But there are things in the house that belong to me. And things we bought together." I was nearly yelling now.

"Do I understand correctly, you haven't worked since moving here? How then could you have 'bought things together' if you had no income?"

"But Eddie said …"

"What Eddie said is in his will which I have in front of me. And there is nothing in it for you."

"But Bob, what am I going to do?" I wailed.

There was a pause, and the scene from *Gone with the Wind* when Scarlett appeals to Rhett Butler flashed in my mind.

Bob quietly hung up.

I was stunned. Not four weeks ago, Bob Franks and his wife Anna, and Eddie and I, had seen a movie together and gone for dessert afterward. What had happened for him to turn against me this way? I had never felt so desperate in my life.

Betty was wrong. I did try to fight. But I don't know who to fight. It was like the kids and their support group had put up a wall around what used to be my life, and I was shut out from it. There was no one to turn to.

Twenty-one

"The hell? Whatcha doing in my shed?" A screechy old voice wakes me with a start. God, I'm trapped.

"Get your sorry ass outta my shed now and be gone with you." An old guy is waving a rake in my face and kicking at my feet. I jump up and out of the way of the rake, looking back to my cart and blanket. I move to reach it, but the rake comes down on my shoulder, hard, and I jump back.

"Git. Git." He chases me a ways down the alley, then stands shouting. "Don't let me catch you around here again. I'll call the cops." Two neighbours come out of their yards to see what the commotion is all about.

"Goddam tramps and bums. Trespassing and thinking the govermunt owes 'em a living. Well, they just better keep offa my property or they'll be sorry." He glares at me once more, then snaps the padlock shut.

Now I'm really screwed. Everything I own is locked in that shed and all I have is some change in my pocket. All my damage deposit money is there, over $800. It's snowing harder now and feels way colder than last night. What do I do now?

I lean against the fence for a while and cry. Then I walk. I don't know where I'm going or where to go. Just keep walking.

The snow is drier now, piling up and starting to drift. I keep to back alleys, where the fences provide a bit of shelter.

Then I'm at the Second Cup, right where Officer Cuba dropped me off yesterday.

I don't have the price of a cup of coffee, but I get in line anyhow. A few people give me unpleasant glares. Then it's my turn.

"Uh, could you just give me 85 cents worth of coffee; I can't buy the whole cup." The girl at the counter starts to protest, then the man behind me steps up.

"For Christ's sake, give her a cup of coffee," as he slams a toonie on the counter. I thank him, grab the cup and head to the door.

"Ma'am, your change ma'am?" The light is green and I cross the freeway, heading west. There's a new building going up where they tore down the old Burger Baron and I squeeze in between a new wall and a stack of lumber. I drink the coffee, black. I wasn't sticking around for cream and sugar after that scene.

Surprisingly, the coffee makes me drowsy and I drift off for a bit.

I'm covered in snow when I wake up. I shake and brush it off and wonder where to go next. I feel unstable without my cart; it was like an extra limb I'd grown and now my balance is off.

Across the street, I see people arriving at the "cell phone" church. This church has one of the highest crosses in the city; rumour has it that it was paid for by a cellular company looking for a place to put a tower. It was a bit of a scandal at the time, this combining of the religious and the commercial, but now that everyone carries cell phones, it's become an urban legend.

Perhaps I'll just join the funeral for a moment or two, warm up a bit at the back of the church.

An usher at the door gives me an odd look, not surprisingly, and asks in a hushed tone, "Family or friend, madame?" I whisper friend, and he leads me to a seat far from the other mourners.

The organ music makes me pensive, and I'm soon drifting again.

Twenty-two

After talking to Bob Franks, I knew the situation was pretty grim. My money was low; I couldn't afford another night at the hotel and I needed to find work. I left my bag at the front desk, promising to come back for it later. The young desk clerk gave me a whatever shrug and went back to her magazine.

There were help wanted signs everywhere and I felt optimistic. Until I got to the end of the application form at a nearby coffee shop. Previous jobs. Current address. Length of residence. Phone number.

Well, shit on a stick, like Eddie used to say. How do you get a job with no phone number? I told the waitress who'd given me the form that I was staying with friends and couldn't take calls there, but I'd come by tomorrow and see about the job. She just shrugged and stuck the application in a drawer at the front desk.

I used the same ploy at the next places I went to, then decided to pick up my bag at the hotel and figure out what to do for the night. The job hunt was humiliating as each person in turn looked suspicious about my evasive excuse for no phone number. I was so feeling so low I didn't see how things could get any worse.

They got way worse, real fast.

There was no sign of my bag at the hotel and the girl I left it with was off shift. I badgered her replacement to look around and to search the little office behind the desk. Nothing. No bag. Her lack of concern made me furious and I began pounding on the desk and yelling. Swearing. The nice security guard from the other day came around the corner with a not-so-nice look on his face.

Out of the corner of my eye, I saw Dan, one of Eddie's friends. He was looking over at the commotion. Before he recognized me, I spun away from the front desk and out the back entrance to avoid running into him. That's all I needed: meeting up with someone I knew, trying to explain what had happened and the situation I now found myself in. I'd die before I'd ask for help; the whole thing was so embarrassing and if Bob wouldn't talk to me, probably the word was out and no one else would either.

My feet wandered aimlessly down the avenue. The sidewalks were empty now of shoppers and sightseers with leashed dogs or baby carriages, and the shops were closing up. The younger crowd was moving in, swaggering, rude, headed for the first beers of the evening. They strode three and four abreast, knocking into me as if I wasn't there. Whyte Avenue was not a good place to be after dark.

I sat at a bus bench and counted my money. Forty dollars. Not enough for even a flea bag hotel. Where would I spend the night?

Aimlessly, I drifted into the Strat, an old hotel bar that catered to everyone from bikers to university students, and ordered a beer. The waiter took my five and asked if I wanted change.

"Of course I do," I snapped, then apologized, saying I had had some bad news and was a bit testy. He returned with my change a few minutes later, but carefully avoided my table as he made his rounds.

Two hours is a long time to nurse a beer, which I don't even particularly like, but at last I decided I'd worn out my welcome. Further on down the avenue, where the bars and coffee shops stop, I reached an apartment block with a street level garage. Thinking it would be a good place to catch some sleep, I went in search of a clean place to lie down.

I found it close to the exit: a small concrete bench-like thing, away from the lights. It looked luxurious to me, I was so tired. I stretched out with my purse for a pillow and fell instantly asleep.

Suddenly, someone was shaking me, yelling. "Hey you. Get up. This here is no hostel or nothing. You gotta get out of here." I stretched achingly to a sitting position; my joints hurt and I was cold. The man in front of me did a double take when he saw my good suit and neat appearance.

"Gee ma'am. Uh, I didn't mean to scare you. But you can't sleep in here. This is private property." He was obviously expecting a bum.

"I'm sorry. I didn't mean any harm. It's just that ..." A lie started to form in my mind. "I am staying here with a friend and I lost the key she gave me, so I'm waiting for her to come home and let me in."

"Well, why didn't you say so? What suite is your friend in? I have a master key; I could phone her cell or something and let you in."

I shook my head and got up. "No, I think I'll just go for a walk. I'll try again later."

Truth was, that beer was sitting heavily on my bladder, and if I didn't pee soon, I'd embarrass myself. I left the parkade in a state of near panic.

There was a ravine nearby. I just hoped I'd make it. And afterwards, I'd find a clean place under a tree or something and sleep a bit more.

That was the morning I met Mr. Taylor and began my life as a bona fide street person.

Twenty-three

I thought the day I met Mr. Taylor, I'd reached the low of lows. But look at me now, hiding in a church at someone's funeral.

The service is strangely comforting, until the eulogist is announced. A young man gets up and begins: "Husband, father, brother, uncle, friend ... no matter how James fit into your life, that life was richer for James being part of it."

My thoughts fly to Eddie, tears began to pour and I quietly leave the church.

As I get myself back together in the bus shelter in front of the church, a bus chugs up, and slides to a stop in the rutted snow. The driver opens the door and waves me on.

"I don't have bus fare."

He gestures toward the empty bus. "Not like you're taking a ride away from a paying customer, is it?" I climb aboard and settle in a seat near the front. The driver makes no attempt at conversation, just maneuvers the bus down the snowy street. When we turn at the road leading to the river valley, I see a crowd of students waiting at the stop across from the high school. I ring the bell for the next stop.

"I go right uptown, y'know. Can drop you by the women's shelter." I shake my head and get off.

There's not much around here; a medical clinic, a strip of stores that don't look like they cater to street bums, which I have to admit describes my circumstances to a tee. Farther up the street is the huge, empty school yard with gusts of snow blowing across. I stick to the north side of the road where the trees provide some shelter from the wind and drifting snow.

I've never been so scared and lonely—and cold—in my life. It's nearly dark now, and my feet are almost hidden from my view in the blowing snow. I'm stumbling downhill; the wind against my face is pure misery. There's a cop car coming up the hill and I duck deeper into the bush. It zooms past, headlights illuminating the thousands of snow flakes drifting down. It seems warmer in the bushes, so I carry on, dodging trees limbs and fallen branches.

A whack across my face nearly knocks me down. I've been so busy watching my footing that I walked smack into tree limb. My nose is bleeding. I pinch the nostrils shut, but it won't stop. My right hand and the blood and my nose start to freeze together and I stumble more because I'm off balance with only one hand to steady myself.

Okay, here's a wire fence, the golf course boundary I guess. I picked Eddie up here after a game one afternoon. I can't climb over the fence with one hand, so I peel my fingers from my nose and struggle over, falling into a drift on the other side. My nose is still bleeding—drip, drip, drip down the front of my jacket.

Now I trip and fall into another drift, feeling dizzy as I struggle to my feet. Maybe it's the nose bleed or that I haven't eaten since the night with Cara.

There's a small hill now, shuffle slowly so I don't fall. What the … the ground goes out from under me and I'm up to my knees in water. Oh god, the water hazard; I thought they drained them in winter. Now I'm wet on top of cold. Have to get out; the water is freezing. I'm out but soaked to my elbows and my feet are in pain.

There's a building up there. The club house? If I can just get there, maybe the wind won't be so bad, and there'll be heat coming off the building. The course is closed, but they'd have to heat the building, wouldn't they? So the water pipes won't freeze? The thought of water reminds me I haven't been to the bathroom since early last night. I feel a trickle down my leg and there's nothing I can do to stop it.

What's this? A lean-to of some kind. That snow drift in the corner looks like a good place to rest. Okay, sit and huddle in, wrap my arms around my knees. My toes won't wiggle. I can't even feel them; they must be frozen.

I'm shivering so hard my teeth rattle. Okay, breathe slowly. There, the shivers slow down and my nose is hardly bleeding any more. Get these runners off; rub some feeling into my toes.

What would Eddie's kids think if they saw me now? Do they ever wonder where I went, what happened to me? Probably not. They went to a lot of trouble to keep me away: freezing bank accounts, canceling credit cards and the home phone and my cell. Oh Eddie, why did you have to die?

Wait a minute. What if he didn't really die? What if his kids just staged a big hoax to get rid of me?

That's it; the obituary was a fake and Eddie's alive, missing me, wondering where I went. They probably told him I left, but he wouldn't believe that. He's probably searching everywhere for me, maybe even has a detective working for him.

He could be on his way over to the golf course right now, and he's probably got a thermos of hot tea and brandy, like the time we went to the football game. Maybe we'll go for dinner and then somewhere to listen to music after. Better get my dirty jacket off and the sweater

I'm wearing; the shirt underneath is cleaner. Wish I had some lipstick, and a comb.

I'm getting sleepy, but I need to stay awake so I hear Eddie when he gets here. Are those car lights turning into the parking lot down there?

Mmm, it's so peaceful here with the big snowflakes drifting down. I feel kind of floaty all over, like after a hot bath. My bundled up jacket and sweater make a nice pillow.

Wait, that's Eddie calling, isn't it? Just down there a ways. It's hard to hear over the wind, but I'm sure that's Eddie. I'd know his voice anywhere. He's calling my name.

"Over here, Eddie." He'll be here in just a minute, and then I'll be warm again. I close my eyes to rest a bit now. Eddie's coming for me.

978-0-595-47473-8
0-595-47473-X

Printed in the United States
108514LV00004BA/1-99/P